AMINATA COOTE

A Family for Christmas

HopeLight
Publishers

For nothing is hidden that will not be made manifest, nor is anything secret that will not be known and come to light.

Luke 8:17 ESV

Contents

1	Chapter 1	1
2	Chapter 2	6
3	Chapter 3	10
4	Chapter 4	18
5	Chapter 5	24
6	Chapter 6	28
7	Chapter 7	33
8	Chapter 8	38
9	Chapter 9	43
10	Chapter 10	49
11	Chapter 11	53
12	Chapter 12	59
13	Chapter 13	64
14	Chapter 14	68
15	Chapter 15	73
16	Chapter 16	79
17	Chapter 17	85
18	Chapter 18	91
19	Chapter 19	98
20	Chapter 20	106
21	Chapter 21	113
22	Chapter 22	119
23	Chapter 23	125
24	Chapter 24	131

25	Chapter 25	137
26	Chapter 26	142
27	Chapter 27	148
28	Chapter 28	153
29	Chapter 29	159
30	Chapter 30	164
31	Chapter 31	169
32	Chapter 32	176
	Epilogue	182
	Author's Note	184
	About the Author	186
	Other Books by the Author	187
	Newsletter Sign-up	189
	Want more inspirational romance?	190

One

Chapter 1

Madison Porter told her twin all her secrets—except one. Her sister wouldn't have approved half the things she'd done because of her big secret, and she craved Mackenzie's approval.

Though Madison was technically older by seven minutes, it was Mackenzie who'd always taken charge, been the "responsible" twin. Not that Madison was irresponsible, but Mackenzie had never met an organizational system she didn't like. Something Madison was thankful for as it made it easier for her to slip into Mackenzie's life as if she'd been tailor-made for it.

Madison grinned at her reflection in the door of The Sweet Tooth before she pulled it open. Since she and Mackenzie were identical twins, she kinda was.

Madison inhaled, filling her lungs with the delicious scents of baked goods. Starting her day with sweets wasn't the smartest thing, but Mackenzie's cupboards were sparse. As in only a few cans of tinned stuff sparse. No way would she start her day eating something out of a can.

She scanned the room. Pastel walls with framed photos of baked goods and small tables and chairs in the lightest gray gave the bakery a whimsical feel. She'd have to exercise if she planned to come here often, and judging by the number of people collecting paper bags and cups, she was in for a treat.

Glad she wasn't the only one with a sweet tooth, Madison suppressed a chuckle, joining the line behind a man who beat a rhythm on his leg. Did he think it would compel the servers to move faster?

Not her problem. She focused instead on the sparkling display case. Should she have a chocolate-covered donut or a glazed one? She tapped her chin. Or maybe she should have a Danish. When was the last time she'd had one of those?

"You can move up in the line."

Madison jumped at the masculine voice too close to her ear.

"Oh." She stepped forward, then turned to say thanks. Her lips froze before they could curve into a smile. It was him. Wasn't it? Her eyes darted over the man, cataloging his features.

He was a couple of inches taller than her, which made him what? About six feet? His lanky frame clad in blue jeans, a plaid shirt, and a leather jacket was surprisingly appealing. The man ran a hand over his beard.

"Do I look that bad?"

Her face burned. "No."

She whirled and stepped into the gap that had opened while she'd been gawking at Xavier Washington. Was it really him?

The man behind her didn't resemble the picture in the newspaper article. That man had worn a suit, his expression stern. This guy was almost approachable, though an air of sadness clung to him.

She stiffened her neck so she wouldn't stare back at him. Was this a sign she was doing the right thing? Or that she wasn't? This would normally have been a praying moment. But Madison had run out of words for the God who'd made it impossible for her to have children after everything she'd already sacrificed.

Madison collected her breakfast and slipped into a seat at the last empty table. She opened the bag and took out the first donut. A morning like this called for two donuts. She sniffed the donut, eyes closing as she savored the smell of fried dough and sugar before taking a huge bite.

"Do you always smell your food?"

Her eyes flew open. Why was he still here? At her table?

"May I?" He gestured to the chair across from her with one hand.

Weren't there other tables with empty seats? Her eyes darted around the room. Nope. Every chair was occupied. Except one. She nodded.

This was what she wanted, wasn't it? A chance to meet Xavier. To get close to him. But she wasn't ready. She'd planned to find out his routine and catch glimpses of him at her leisure. She hadn't planned to interact with him. And she certainly hadn't intended to stumble over him in a bakery.

"Thanks." He dropped into the chair, eyes closing briefly.

Madison frowned at him. Was he praying? Somehow, she hadn't expected that of him. But then, stalking a man online didn't mean you knew anything about them. Especially not when there was so little information to uncover.

"Do you?"

She blinked. What were they talking about?

He tipped his chin toward the donut. "Always sniff your food."

"Oh." She glanced down at the donut that she'd smashed between her fingers. Why was she eating here again? "No."

The corners of his lips tipped upward. He'd appeared grim before, but the smile transformed his face into an interesting one. A ping of something zapped through her too fast for her to identify the emotion.

"Do you always talk in monosyllables?"

"No."

He sighed, returning his croissant to the bag. "I'm sorry. I'll leave you alone." He pushed back his chair.

"No!" She clutched at his arm before he stood. If she let him get away now, it would destroy this perfect opportunity she had to get to know him better. His eyes dropped to her hand.

"Sorry." She released him and moistened her lips. "You don't have to go."

His brow furrowed. "Are you sure?"

She nodded. Maybe if she didn't talk…

"I'm Xavier." He stuck a hand across the table.

"I know who you are."

His eyebrows shot up. Madison's face burned.

Keep going, Madison, way to make a first impression on the guy. He'd believe she was some kind of stalker.

You kinda are. The tiny voice in the back of her head piped up. Was she the only person whose inner voice needed a timeout?

"You have a daughter who's into video games?"

As a video game designer, he wasn't exactly on the cutting edge of Saturn Island society. Why hadn't she planned this out before? Figured out what she would say if she'd, somehow, captured his attention?

"No. I," she looked down at the paper bag, running her fingers over the grease marks. "I read a newspaper article about you moving to Orange Valley."

It had been the catalyst for her twin switch proposition with Mackenzie. Not that her sister had wanted to switch places.

"Okay." Xavier took a sip from his cup. "Then you have me at a disadvantage."

"Sorry?" Did he always talk that way? With gigantic gaps in his conversation. Or was she less inclined to focus on what he was saying because her thoughts were so loud?

"You haven't told me your name."

"Oh." She jolted. "Mad-Mackenzie."

He frowned. "Mad Mackenzie?"

She stifled a groan. He must think she was the stupidest woman on earth.

"No, just Mackenzie." Her tongue didn't stumble over her sister's name this time. "Mackenzie Porter." In case he assumed she was one of those one-name sensations.

He smiled. He had a beautiful smile. One that had nothing to do with the straight white teeth but with the kindness it exuded.

Xavier Washington seemed to be a nice person. And if he was a nice guy, that would make her the villain in this story.

Two

Chapter 2

Xavier Washington wasn't sure why he'd crashed her table. Possibly because, for one second, the awareness in her gaze had sparked emotions that had been lying dormant for the past three years. Curiosity. Interest. Loneliness.

It had been a long time since he'd had a conversation about something other than his loss or Gracie's care. Or had wanted to.

Wasn't that what moving to Orange Valley was about? An opportunity to shake himself out of the rut he'd been living in since his wife, Alicia, had died?

Had he hoped this woman was the first step to bridging the barrier he'd erected between himself and the rest of humanity? He took a sip of his lemongrass tea. He'd made a mistake. What he should have done was stick to the plan.

It had been simple enough. Eat his croissant in the car while waiting for the school to open. Register Gracie, and return home where he'd sequester himself in his office, pretending to work until Gracie sought him out.

That's what he'd do now. He repackaged his croissant and pushed back his chair. "I'm sorry. I'll leave you alone."

The woman clutched at his arm. For the second time that morning, he experienced an unfamiliar emotion. His gaze dropped to the long fingers that gripped him. Fingers with a strength that shouldn't exist in this slender woman.

What was it about her that resurrected all these emotions? And why did he want to stay in her presence to discover what other emotions awakened?

He settled back into the chair and considered the woman across from him. Nervous energy buzzed around her. He studied her, trying to puzzle it out.

Maybe she was embarrassed because she'd recognized him from a grainy photo taken over four years ago. He stroked his beard. A photo that was so unlike the image greeting him in the mirror these days that he couldn't reconcile the two as being of the same man. An uncomfortable silence settled between them.

Nice going, Xavier. You ruined this poor woman's breakfast. And his own, because his appetite had fled. He should pack up his breakfast and escape to the safety of his vehicle, where he never had to worry about awkward conversations.

But what would be the point of that? He'd come to Orange Valley for a fresh start. One that pushed him outside his comfort zone. Was there anything more uncomfortable than talking to a strange woman? A woman who'd made him acknowledge his loneliness.

"What's there to do in Orange Valley?"

"Why did you move to Orange Valley?"

They spoke simultaneously, their words overlapping.

"Go ahead." He gestured for her to repeat her question, though if he'd heard her correctly, he'd prefer not to answer.

She cleared her throat. "Why Orange Valley?"

Yup. Not a question that was a suitable conversation with someone he'd just met. Especially since he hadn't discussed it with anyone in his family. He scanned her expression. Curiosity and a hint of sadness met his gaze.

Had this woman gone through a smidgen of the grief he'd been battling with for the past three years? And wouldn't this be a perfect opportunity to test if he was ready to come from behind his walls? Because who better to share your secrets with than a complete stranger?

The silence became interminable until Mackenzie dropped her gaze.

"Never mind." She shredded the donut between her fingers. "Forget I said anything."

His eyes dropped to the mangled pile of dough in front of her. He could do this. He forced the words out.

"I came here so my daughter and I could start fresh, without the death of my wife hanging over us."

Well, that was blunt, and probably the end of this impromptu tea party.

"I'm sorry for your loss."

He believed her. The emotions that swirled in the depths of her brown eyes were too deep to be faked. He gave a curt nod, unsure how to respond. Most people expected him to move on with his life. After all, it had been over three years.

As far as everyone else was concerned, Alicia was dead and buried and he should get over it. Forget about the five years they'd been married or the seven years they'd been together.

They wanted him to forget that she'd died while he had lived. That he had to raise their daughter without her. Or that her family looked at him as if they wondered why he was alive and their precious daughter was not.

He shook his head. Get a hold of yourself, Xavier. At the rate he was going, he'd start bawling in his tea. Wouldn't that create an impression on the pretty woman and everyone in the store?

"What's there to do at Christmas around here?"

He'd chosen Christmas since people were kinder during the holidays, and they'd integrate into the community more easily. For now, his sister-in-law helped him and Gracie settle in, but she wouldn't stay forever. Soon, Jacqui would return to Idlewood and it would be him and Gracie.

"Uhm," she cast her gaze around. "I'm not really sure."

He frowned. "Are you new in town, too?"

Her laugh had a nervous edge. "I'm usually not in Orange Valley for Christmas."

"Oh." He'd have to ask someone else then. The thought of speaking to another person that day had sweat running down his back. Oh, brother. When had he become a recluse?

Before Alicia's death, he had liked people and thrived on interaction. Now, not as much. If he didn't speak to anyone other than Gracie for weeks, he was ecstatic.

That stopped now. Gracie deserved more than a dad who hid away from the world. He wasn't quite ready to lead any parades, but he was definitely done with hiding away from everyone.

"Where can I find a church?"

Three

Chapter 3

Madison slipped into the back pew of Hope Church on Wednesday evening. It had been months since she'd been in a church and she waited for something. A voice to tell her she wasn't welcome there? An unkind glare? Anything to give her the justification to leave.

Instead, everyone's attention remained on the praise and worship team on the platform. The voices of the three women blended perfectly with the lone male's, but she tuned them out before she could feel anything.

She refused to think about how alone she felt without her faith to sustain her. Or about how often she started praying before she remembered she no longer did that.

What was she doing there, anyway? Just because she'd recommended her sister's church to Xavier was no reason for her to be there herself. Her eyes darted to the entrance. If she left now, she'd be back at Mackenzie's in less than fifteen minutes.

She was halfway off the bench when a pretty woman in braids took the stage. Madison blinked at her. Were those blue braids in her hair?

"Have you ever felt as if God had abandoned you?" The woman scanned the crowd and for one second, locked eyes with Madison. "You're praying and asking Him for one thing." She held up a finger. "Something so simple you know He can do it. But," the woman shrugs, "there's only silence. Not a single word from the Creator."

Yes. Madison's heart screamed as her butt dropped back into the pew.

"Multiply your emotions by four hundred years," the woman continued, "and you may have an idea of how the Israelites felt during the intertestamental period."

Madison no longer wanted to leave. Instead, she sat and listened to the sermon. This woman had reached into her mind—into the deepest recesses of her heart—and pulled out the pain she was wrestling with.

How could a God who loved her allow her to go through such pain? Why did He keep taking when He had the ability to bless?

She pondered the questions as the congregation stood for the final prayer. Was there something wrong with her? Had she somehow displeased or dishonored God and lost His favor?

"Mackenzie?"

A hand rested on her forearm, and she jumped. Her eyes darted around the sanctuary. How had she gone from wanting to leave to being the last person left?

"Are you okay?" Concern brimmed from the woman who'd spoken the words that had pierced her heart.

"Yes. I'm fine. Powerful message, by the way." Just because the woman had cast an enormous stone into her glass house was no reason not to give her credit for her poignant presentation.

"Thanks." The woman made a face. "People assume because I'm a pastor's wife, I don't have times when I wrestle with my faith."

This was the pastor's wife? Madison tried not to gape.

"Anyway," the woman clapped her hands. "That's not why I came to you."

Her eyebrows shot up. What could this woman have to talk to her about? But then, she wasn't really talking to Madison, was she? She believed she was talking to Mackenzie. Madison squirmed.

She'd forgotten this aspect of switching places with her sister—having expectations put on her she hadn't made. It had been fun in high school. Now, it was torturous.

"Please tell me you're not working this holiday." The woman's plea was reflected in her eyes.

Had her sister ever mentioned the name of the pastor's wife? Madison scrolled through her memory, struggling to hold a conversation without the woman realizing Madison had no idea who she was.

"Mackenzie?" The woman prompted.

She'd been silent too long. "No. I'm free until after the first of the year." Madison parroted what Mackenzie had told her.

"Oh, good." The woman's eyes glowed with glee and a hint of mischief. "I need your help."

"Mine?" Madison pressed a palm to her chest. Had her sister made plans and forgotten to tell her about them?

"Yes." The pastor's wife slipped onto the pew beside Madison, angling toward her. "We're hosting a VBS—vacation Bible school—and need more volunteers."

The woman made a face. "It was very last minute as we hadn't planned to host one, but several parents came to us," she lifted a shoulder. "It was hard to say no." Her eyes lifted to Madison's, a hint of desperation in their depths. "Can you help?"

No! The word echoed so loudly in her mind it was a wonder the pastor's wife hadn't heard it. The last place she should be was around children. Why wallow in the reminder of everything she couldn't have?

Yes, her heart whispered, already conjuring images of little arms wrapped around her neck and the joy of spending a few hours every day with children.

"Please?" The woman clasped her hands and pouted her lips in the perfect imitation of a child. "It's only Mondays to Thursdays for two weeks."

"Just say no." An elegant woman swooped onto the bench beside the pastor's wife. Was this the woman's mother? "Don't let Brianna talk you into anything."

Brianna. Madison latched on the woman's name like a lifeline. Brianna turned a mock scowl at the older woman. "Leave me alone, Grace. Aren't you supposed to be helping me recruit?"

"Recruit, not coerce." Grace's eyes twinkled.

Madison's gaze darted between the two women, sensing an underlying conversation but having no way to interpret it.

"Well?" Brianna's brown eyes focused on Madison. "Will you help us?"

"Uh—"

"Don't answer yet," Brianna rushed to speak. "Think about it and tell me tomorrow. If you decide to help, we start Monday and will be here from nine to twelve." She stood.

"Let's go, Grace." Brianna pulled the older woman to her feet. "I can't have you talking her out of it before she gets the chance to decide for herself. I'll see you tomorrow."

Brianna waggled her fingers at Madison and then tugged Grace deeper into the sanctuary with her.

Madison shuffled out of the pew, intent on escaping before someone else approached, asking her to volunteer for another task.

* * *

For the first time ever, Madison didn't decorate for Christmas. She knew where her sister kept the ornaments but wasn't in the mood to do Christmas. Madison stretched out on the sofa, a bowl of buttery popcorn on the floor beside her. She flipped through the channels to find a non-Christmas movie. A vehicle pulled up outside, and she muted the television.

The only person who knew she was here was Mackenzie. She stifled a groan. What if someone came to Mackenzie? She didn't feel up to playing her twin right now.

She wanted to watch a movie and eat her popcorn while she tried to forget Brianna's request. Several minutes ticked by, but no one came to the door. Had the person left?

She crept to the window overlooking the yard and shifted the curtain to peer outside. There was a vehicle parked at the gate and someone was inside. Why didn't they come to the door? Were they lost? Was she in danger?

Madison rushed back to the sofa for her cell phone. She had just clasped it when there was a rap at the door. She exhaled a sigh of relief. A burglar or someone who planned to hurt her wouldn't knock, would they?

She peeked through the peephole and gawked. Cameron Grant stood on her front step. The real estate developer had become a local sensation after taking over his parents' firm at eighteen and propelling it into an empire. Why was he here?

Wait, wasn't he one of Mackenzie's clients? She tensed. Did the tycoon expect Mackenzie to work this holiday? How did her sister's job work, anyway?

Open the door, Madison. She wouldn't get any answers until she did. Her sister would never forgive her if she cost Mackenzie her cushy job as an air attendant. She cracked open the door.

"Yes?"

The man exuded power and she had to steel herself against being intimidated. How did Mackenzie work with him without quaking in her boots?

"May I come in?"

She scanned him from head to toe before huffing out a breath. She didn't really have a choice, did she? Not while she was pretending to be Mackenzie. She stepped back, allowing him entry.

His gaze scanned the room. What did this place look like through his eyes? She tilted her chin. She had nothing to be ashamed of. And neither did Mackenzie. The room was clean, with no clutter in sight.

The grandfather clock had been one of the few projects Mackenzie had done by herself. She'd bought it at a garage sale and painstakingly restored the old clock until it was in pristine condition. His quiet scrutiny was making her nervous. She tapped her foot.

"Well?"

"Do you know why I'm here?"

Her eyebrows shot up. Had Mackenzie sent him? "Why would I know that?"

He shifted his stance, and his unsettling gray eyes zoomed in on her. Her mouth dried. The woman who became the focus of this man's attention had to be strong indeed.

"You don't?"

Cameron Grant pressed into her personal space, his bulk and height making her feel small. She stiffened her spine, refusing to cower.

"Ever since that kiss we shared on your last shift, I can't stop thinking about you."

Her eyes widened. Mackenzie had kissed him? What had her sister been thinking? She raised both hands to fend him off.

"Mr. Grant!"

Cameron Grant backed up. "So you do know who I am."

"Yes, Mr. Grant. I've been working for you for the past eighteen months."

He arched a brow. What had she gotten herself into?

"Look." Madison swiped a hand over her hair. "I shouldn't have kissed you." And if her sister had kissed him, *she* would not.

She exhaled, pushing every thought out of her head except for one. She had to get him out of there.

"It was unprofessional and I'm sorry. I hope you won't hold it against me and it won't affect our relationship."

Oh, brother. Was her sister in a relationship with this man? If she was, why hadn't she said anything? Hurt frizzled through Madison but she couldn't process that now.

"You admit that we have a relationship?"

He grinned and Madison understood what her sister saw in Cameron Grant. He was handsome, but he would not mess up her plans. She firmed her voice.

"A professional one." She raised a hand. "You and I have a professional relationship that will remain that way."

She mentally patted herself on the back. Her limbs were like noodles, but she hadn't stuttered or trembled once.

"Who are you and what have you done with Mackenzie?"

She sputtered. Had she said something to expose her secret?

"Nothing." Her eyes widened as she realized what she'd said. "I mean, I'm Mackenzie." She patted her chest. Maybe if she were more emphatic, he'd believe her. "Mackenzie Porter, that's who I am."

She straightened to her full height, mimicking the haughty expression her sister sometimes used to keep people at a distance. "You should leave now, Mr. Grant."

"Gladly." He pivoted, pausing beside the door, resting a palm on the doorjamb.

"Mackenzie?"

"Hmm?" Why wouldn't he leave? She was at the end of her composure.

"What's your sister's name?"

"Madison." She clapped a hand over her mouth. How had he known she had a sister? Was there something going on between the billionaire and her sister? Was that why Mackenzie had allowed herself to be talked into a switch?

Something was up with Kenzie, but what? She heaved a sigh of relief when the door clicked shut behind Cameron Grant, and made a mental note to call her sister later. But first, she had to decide how she'd answer Brianna's question.

Four

Chapter 4

Xavier held his breath as he slipped into the house. Maybe he could get to his office without talking to Jacqui.

"Xavier?"

He exhaled a breath. No such luck. He followed Jacqui's voice to the kitchen. His sister-in-law wore an apron over her shapeless house dress.

"Hey, Jacqui."

"I'm making lunch. It's almost ready." She lifted eyes that always reminded him of an over-eager puppy.

He dropped his gaze to the assortment of sliced vegetables and picked up a carrot stick. Not for the first time, his conscience pricked him. He depended on this unassuming woman too much.

"How was today?" She tucked a hank of hair behind her ear.

"Okay. Gracie's registered for the January term. I met her

teacher today and believe they'll get along fine."

"I could have done that, you know."

"You've already done too much for us."

"It's my pleasure. I enjoy taking care of you and Gracie." She smiled and, for a second, he detected something more than fraternal love in her eyes. He blinked, and it disappeared.

"Where's Gracie?" He cast his gaze around the kitchen. Where was his daughter when he needed her help to extricate him from an uncomfortable situation?

"She's having screen time." Jacqui turned to stir the big pot on the stove and the savory smell of pumpkin beef soup filled the air. "She has a half an hour left. By then, this will be ready."

Jacqui swept the vegetables into the pot, and a wave of helplessness washed over Xavier. How would he and Gracie survive without her?

Maybe he should marry Jacqui. Shame pulsed through him. No. He believed in love. What he'd had with Alicia had been precious. He would not cheapen her memory or rob her sister of the chance to be loved the way she deserved to be.

"I'll check on her."

Xavier paused at the door of the living room to gaze at his beautiful daughter.

"You're staring at me, Daddy."

He grinned. "I am?"

"You are. Why?"

"Because you're the most beautiful girl in the world."

She turned to him, head tilted. "You're not supposed to say that."

"No?" He drew closer, curious about her answer.

She shook her head. "No. The most beautiful girl in the world is the one you love. Like Mommy. And if I get a new mommy, then she should be the most beautiful girl in the world to you."

"Uh—" She wanted a new mommy? Where had she gotten these ideas?

"You can call me the most beautiful daughter in the world. Unless you have another one. Then we'll both be the most beautiful."

How was he supposed to respond to these pearls of wisdom that seemed to come from a much older source? He made light of it, pretending her words hadn't rocked his world.

"Is that how it works?"

She nodded, face solemn. "Sit here." She patted the seat beside him.

He glanced at the screen, frowning at the identical girls on the screen when he'd been expecting a cartoon.

"What are you watching?"

"It Takes Two." She kept her eyes fixed on the television. "I wish I had a twin, don't you?"

"When did you start watching movies?" What he really wanted to know was when she'd grown up on him. Had he been so wrapped in his grief he'd neglected his daughter?

"Oh, Daddy," she sounded older than her five years. "I've been watching this show for ages." Her eyes shone with amusement. "You should create twin characters for your next game."

He made a noncommittal noise. His creativity had dried up with Alicia's death, and it had been three years since he'd created a game. Yet another reason for the move. Maybe the new environment would revive his muse. There were a lot of expectations tied to this address change.

God, will any of these dreams come true?

Prayer had become habitual, though he'd long given up on

hearing from God. He clung to the ashes of his faith because he had nothing else left.

The last Bible study he'd done before Alicia died had been on the life of David. If the shepherd-turned-king could cling to his faith in the middle of everything he'd gone through, then Xavier would do the same. He was just waiting for God to show up for him as He had for David.

* * *

"Xavier?" Jacqui called softly as she tapped on his office door. Jacqui always announced her presence, afraid to interrupt. Unlike Alicia, who would have burst into the room and demanded all attention for herself.

"Are you busy?"

He sighed and locked the computer. Better for his sister-in-law not to find out he'd been playing solitaire under the guise of working.

"You may come in."

Jacqui entered on soft feet. She'd exchanged the shapeless dress for an oversized t-shirt and baggy shorts that hung to her knees. She'd scraped her hair into a ponytail.

"Gracie's asleep."

Guilt flooded him. Hadn't he promised himself that he'd do a better job of caring for his daughter? Shouldn't that include being present at bedtime?

"Thanks." He cleared his throat and gestured to the sofa in the gaming area. The plush couch was in front of a large screen that was connected to several game consoles. He followed her and perched at the opposite end of the couch.

"Gracie's adjusting well."

"Yes." He waited with a sense of foreboding.

"As you know, I can work from anywhere."

Her job as a medical coder was as flexible as his, which is why their arrangement had worked well. He nodded.

"You've been a tremendous help since Alicia—" He refused to say the word. There had been too much emotional upheaval today.

Jacqui stared down at her hands. "I was considering staying until after the new year. Until Gracie's settled in school."

An image flashed in his head, him and Jacqui keeping house as Gracie grew older. Two lives on hold because they couldn't move past the death of a loved one.

"No." She jolted at his harsh tone. He gentled his voice. "Thank you, but no."

She'd already given up three years of her life. For three years, she'd stepped in as Gracie's caregiver, sometimes her primary caregiver. She'd cooked meals, cleaned his house, washed his clothes, and for what reason? Because he'd been too grief-stricken to pick up the threads of his life after his wife had died?

"We talked about this. Gracie and I need to figure out how to be a family without," he swallowed hard. "Without everyone swooping in." Alicia's parents and his had agreed that a new town would be a fresh start for him and Gracie.

The only dissenter had been Jacqui. Not that she'd said a word, but her sad eyes had communicated her disapproval as clearly as if she'd used a megaphone.

"I don't mind." Her fingers twisted and untwisted in her lap.

"Jacqui," he said her name softly and waited until she met his gaze. "You've put your life on hold long enough."

"I'd do anything for you." Her voice came out low and

passionate.

Uh-oh. His earlier apprehension was back. Amplified.

"Don't you see?" Her eyes roamed over his face, earnestness exuding from every cell. "I love—"

He flinched, and she sucked in a breath.

"Gracie. I love Gracie."

Somehow, he didn't think that was what she'd meant to say. Had he encouraged her? He cleared his throat. "I know you do."

He wanted to cover her hand with his but feared that would be misleading. How could he have been oblivious to her feelings all these years? He wouldn't make light of it. Xavier chose his next words with care.

"These past three years would have been impossible to get through without you. Gracie has enjoyed having her aunt around and…"

How could he tell her he considered her a sister without insulting her?

"Alicia would have appreciated how you cared for us in her absence."

Her eyes filled, and he braced himself for her tears. He'd never been good at handling female tears.

"I understand." She licked her lips and lowered her head. "I'll leave in the morning. I'll pack my things now."

He exhaled, shoulders sagging with relief as she left the room. Things could have gone a lot worse. He was glad he'd set up the expectation that he wouldn't be home for Christmas as he and Gracie created their own rituals for the season.

There was only one problem. Now that his live-in babysitter was leaving, who would take care of Gracie?

Five

Chapter 5

Madison stopped inside the church door. She'd stayed away for four days. Four excruciatingly long days while Brianna's request played in a loop in her mind.

This morning, she'd convinced herself she'd just check on the vacation Bible school as they should have gotten more than enough volunteers.

The sanctuary was empty and for a second, there was a stirring in her spirit, inviting her back to God.

What was she doing here?

She didn't want to do this—didn't want to spend her vacation caring for other people's children.

Madison had switched places with Mackenzie so she *wouldn't* have to be around children for the holidays. Not after the doctor's PCOS diagnosis had shattered her dream of one day having a family.

"I shouldn't have come here." She whirled and collided with something hard. "Oof."

Hands grabbed her shoulders to steady her. "Are you alright?"

She almost groaned at the familiar voice. Why did she keep bumping into Xavier Washington?

"Fine." She tugged away from his grasp and took a step back. "What are you doing here?"

Her voice came out harsher than she'd intended, but something about this man made her unbalanced. Xavier's eyes cut to his left. She followed his gaze.

Oh. She was beautiful. Madison's eyes brimmed with tears and she resisted the urge to stuff her hands in her mouth to stifle the sob that threatened to escape.

"You're staring at me the way Daddy does."

"Oh?" She cleared the huskiness from her throat. "How is that?"

Madison's gaze roamed over the little girl, committing everything to memory. Delicate features, bow-shaped mouth, mismatched socks.

The child's lips tipped up into a smile. "As if I'm the most beautiful daughter in the world."

Before Madison recovered from the shaft of pain the child's words caused, the little girl peered up at her father.

"You should marry her, Daddy. Then she'll be the most beautiful girl in the world to you."

Marry him? Madison's whole body burned at the idea. Did Xavier think she wanted to marry him? Her eyes shot to him.

"Alana Grace." Xavier's voice was gruff. His attention focused on his daughter. "What did we say about keeping some of our thoughts inside?"

Alana Grace dropped her gaze. "I'm sorry, Daddy."

"Apologize to Ms. Mackenzie."

Alana Grace squirmed. "I'm sorry. I didn't mean to make you feel bad." She looked at her father. "Can I go now?"

Xavier nodded, and the child ran across the sanctuary, disappearing through what must be the entrance to the Children's Department.

Xavier scraped a hand over his beard. "Sorry. Gracie says exactly what's on her mind."

"It's okay." Madison dragged her eyes away from the direction the little girl had gone and focused on Xavier. "I suppose it's important to always tell the truth." She stifled a wince at the hypocrisy of her words. "I should go." She moved to step around him.

"Are you a volunteer?"

"Uh—" her thoughts vacillated between freedom and spending more time with Alana Grace.

"Mackenzie." Her sister's name rang out across the sanctuary and Madison turned. Brianna was making a beeline toward her.

"I'm glad you came." The pastor's wife slung her arms around Madison's shoulders like they were long-lost friends. "Please tell me you're here to help."

Wait, was her sister friends with Brianna? If they were, this would not end well. The key to pulling off a switch was to avoid intimate acquaintances of the other twin. But with Brianna clinging to her and Xavier looking at her as if she were the answer to a prayer, how would she extricate herself?

Lord, if You can hear me, some help, please?

She waited for a second. Would God respond to her frantic plea? Nothing happened. The sky didn't open. No one came to distract Brianna and Xavier. Nothing. Once again, she was on her own to solve her problems. She huffed out a breath and opened her mouth to decline.

"I guess I am." She glanced at Xavier before shifting her attention to Brianna. "Where did you need me?"

"Can you help with the five-year-olds?" Brianna's smile was innocent. As if she hadn't given Madison her greatest desire and her worst nightmare at once.

Six

Chapter 6

How did anyone learn anything from YouTube videos? Xavier glared at the pot of porridge-like rice and then scowled at the frozen face of the cheerful woman who'd insisted cooking was easy.

This was his fault. Xavier had resisted his mother's efforts to teach him to cook. He'd refused even the mention of cooking after his first attempt hadn't resulted in perfection. He'd resisted all her efforts to convince him that cooking was a skill that improved with practice.

He'd left his parents' home and married Alicia. After his wife's death, Jacqui had cooked for them. He'd never prepared a full meal on his own.

"It's okay, Daddy." Gracie patted his hand, her expression compassionate. "Miss M'kenzie says we should keep trying when things are hard. I tried really hard to get my handprint right, but she had to help me."

Gracie had come home from Vacation Bible School with "Miss M'kenzie said" on her lips. If he had a dollar for every time she'd said it, he'd have enough to buy one of his video games.

"I'm sorry, Gracie. We'll be having takeout again."

As they had most evenings since Jacqui left. There was still some soup left in the freezer, but he wanted something different. Besides, he could do without another culinary fail this evening.

"Can we have pizza this time?"

"Sure." Dejection rounded his shoulders. He needed to do better than this, to *be* better for his little girl. "Get your jacket."

He waited until she'd skipped out of the room before lifting his eyes heavenward.

"How long will you ignore me, God? Why won't You answer?"

His voice broke, and he pressed his lips together as he wrestled his emotions under control.

"I need Your help because there's no one else who can help me."

Five minutes later, Gracie clung to his hand, her words going a mile a minute. He'd insisted they walk the short distance to the pizza parlor. If they were going to live on junk food, they'd at least get some exercise.

This couldn't continue much longer, though. Should he hire a housekeeper? Except…wasn't the whole point of moving to Orange Valley to become self-sufficient?

Gracie tugged on his hand. "Look, Daddy." She pointed to a slender woman, wearing a knit coat the colors of autumn. "There's Miss M'kenzie."

"Miss M'kenzie." His daughter's voice had several people

turning. "Come on, Daddy."

She pulled him toward the woman.

"Gracie, maybe we should—"

Gracie dropped his hand and ran toward the woman who was about to slip into a building. Gracie threw her arms around Mackenzie, who tucked the child against her, eyes darting around until they locked on him.

There was a definite zing as their eyes connected. Alright then. He headed toward her. Why did he have a physical reaction every time he saw her?

He kept his eyes on her as he approached. "Hello."

She swallowed. "Hi."

"Why are you here?" He blurted the words and then wanted to smack himself.

The corner of her lips quirked. "I was hungry and didn't want to cook." She pointed at the building behind her.

Xavier tipped his head backward to read the sign. Ruby's Place.

"How about you? Why are you and Gracie roaming the streets when you should be inside, where it's warm?"

Gracie danced from one foot to the next. "Daddy made rice porridge."

Mackenzie wrinkled her nose. "For dinner?"

"Well," Xavier cleared his throat. "I didn't set out to make porridge, more that the rice *came out* as porridge."

Her lips curved. "Didn't something similar happen in the Bible?"

Was she teasing him? It had been a long time since anyone had bothered to coax humor from him.

"Yes, well—"

"We're having pizza!"

Gracie's exuberance made him pause. Was he doing the best thing for her? Alicia had fed her organic foods, soft fruits, and vegetables that she'd pureed herself. Jacqui had continued the trend by providing wholesome, home-cooked meals.

Even Alicia's parents and his had monitored the amount of processed food Gracie ate. Yet under his care, she'd already had more junk in her system than she'd had in the past two years.

Disapproval flashed across Mackenzie's face. His shoulders sagged. He deserved it. He was a failure as a dad.

Mackenzie bent until her face was close to Gracie's. "You can always have dinner with me." Her eyes briefly met his. "I can't promise they'll have pizza, but the food's always good."

Gracie studied Mackenzie in her solemn way. "It's probably not good for me to have too much fast food. Aunt Jacqui always said eating junk food was like putting garbage in your car's fuel tank."

Gracie scrunched up her face. "I'm not sure what that means, but it sounds disgusting."

Xavier stared at Mackenzie in wonder. Why hadn't he suggested they eat at a restaurant that cooked actual food?

"Daddy," Gracie sidled up and took his hand. "We should eat with Miss M'kenzie. We can have pizza another night."

"Okay, Gracie." Xavier's heart overflowed with love for his daughter. What had he done to deserve such a well-adjusted child?

Guilt threatened to overwhelm him once again, and he swallowed hard. No, he would not wallow in self-pity anymore. He was drawing a line in the sand and stepping over it. The old Xavier was gone, and he'd forge a path for a brighter future for himself and Gracie.

He cleared his throat and addressed Mackenzie. "Thank you for inviting us to have dinner with you."

Mackenzie gave him a curt nod before taking Gracie's hand. When she looked at Gracie, her entire demeanor softened. "Shall we?"

Xavier scrambled to open the door for them. Something he'd said or done had tainted Mackenzie's opinion of him. It was evident in the stiffness of her shoulders, in the disapproving press of her lips.

Well, she couldn't be any more disappointed in him than he was in himself. He took a moment to scan the interior rather than obsess over her apparent disapproval or why it mattered.

A long oblong-shaped bar dominated one wall. Most of the seats were full. How many people were there because they didn't know the first thing about preparing a meal for themselves? How many more were there for the company?

"Let's grab one of those tables." Mackenzie gestured to a white-covered table near the back. There were only a few empty chairs.

"Is it always this full?" She may not want to talk with him, ignoring him in favor of Gracie, but he was curious.

She nodded. "Every time I'm here."

"Food must be good."

"We won't find out if we stand here." Gracie grabbed his hand. "Come on, Daddy."

He chuckled and allowed her to drag him deeper into the restaurant.

Seven

Chapter 7

Madison clenched and unclenched her fists as she followed Xavier and Gracie deeper into the restaurant. Pizza for dinner? Okay, so she wasn't against the occasional treat. Her parents had allowed her, Mackenzie, and RJ to have fast food when they were younger, but it had been for special occasions.

From the sound of things, junk food was a staple in their lives. Didn't Xavier understand he was the keeper of his daughter's health? That the choices he made now would have effects stretching way into the future?

She slid into the chair Xavier held out for her, ignoring the twinge of awareness from being this close to him. She plucked up the menu and flipped to the children's section.

"Is there anything she's allergic to or won't eat?" Her eyes flicked to Xavier.

"Uh." He massaged the back of his neck. "I don't think she

has any food allergies."

Her eyebrows shot up. "You don't *think*?" Did this man know anything about his child? That first time they'd met, she'd believed he was a capable father, but now she wasn't so sure.

Examine the full picture before you form an opinion.

"She hates broccoli," Xavier continued, "but loves carrots."

Madison shifted her attention to Gracie, who sat on a chair between them. "You don't like broccoli?" Her heart pounded as she waited for the answer.

"Nope." Gracie shook her head. "Tastes as bad as medicine. Aunt Jacqui says it's all in my head." Gracie lowered her voice to a loud whisper. "She doesn't understand."

Madison hid a smile. "I'll tell you a secret." She leaned closer to Gracie. "I agree with you. Broccoli is the worst food in the world but carrots are delicious."

Xavier groaned. "Thanks, Mackenzie. Now I'll never convince her to take another bite."

Madison shrugged. "There are other vegetables. Focus on giving her those."

She dismissed the twinge of guilt for her snooty tone. "Aunt Jacqui is a big part of your life." Madison imagined an old woman wearing outdated house dresses and an awful wig.

"Jacqui is my wife's younger sister." Sadness crept over his face. "She's been helping with Gracie since Alicia's…"

Oh. She'd forgotten. How had she gotten so caught up in her own pain she'd forgotten he was wrestling with his own?

"I'd love to meet her and show her what Gracie has been working on."

No, Madison, you should not be digging yourself deeper into this family than you already are.

"Maybe. Jacqui went home. I'm not sure when she'll be back."

His tone hinted at something, and she studied his face. What was going on between him and Jacqui? She shook her head. Not her business. The only interest she had in Xavier was his connection to Gracie.

His pain over the death of his wife or whatever was brewing between him and his sister-in-law was none of her concern.

"I'm not sure how Gracie and I will manage without her." He shifted in his chair. "We've grown dependent. Jacqui did most of the cooking and so far, my attempts have been laughable."

Oh. That explained why he was struggling to prepare proper meals for Gracie.

"Why don't you hire a housekeeper?"

He sighed. "I need to learn how to take care of my daughter, without depending on someone to perform basic chores for us."

He smiled at Gracie before his eyes jumped back to hers. "Maybe I should take parenting classes or something."

"You don't need parenting classes, Daddy. You need cooking classes."

Xavier touched one of the girl's twists. "Someone has to teach me how to do these pretty hairstyles you love."

"I can help." Madison stifled a groan as both turned to stare at her. Why hadn't she suggested a hairdresser? Or find out if the church offered parenting classes or would arrange one?

"You can?"

Xavier's face lit up, and once again she had an inclination to get closer to him. What would it take for him to have the same single-minded devotion to her as he had to his dead wife?

What kind of sick woman would think of something like that? The man grieved for his wife. He needed to learn how to take care of his child. He didn't have time for romance, and neither did she.

She was in Orange Valley to find out more about Xavier and get closer to him—er, Gracie. Get closer to Gracie. She should focus on Gracie.

* * *

The next afternoon, Madison stared at herself in the mirror. What would Mackenzie do? She met her gaze and pretended it was her sister's.

"What should I do, Mackenzie?" She addressed her reflection.

Cancel. Nothing good can come from this.

Madison whirled away, ignoring the too-loud voice of her conscience. There was no Vacation Bible School that day, and she'd had made plans with Xavier for an impromptu cooking lesson during Gracie's nap time. Had it already been a week since she'd been helping with the children?

She tugged on her autumn-colored coat over the plum knit dress which she wore over black leggings. An outfit she'd convinced herself she'd worn for comfort and not because it flattered her figure.

She began a brisk walk to Xavier's house as she stuffed her conscience into the deepest recesses of her mind.

She was just spending a few hours helping a neighbor. That's it. She was being neighborly. A good Samaritan. Because it was Christmas, and she hated the idea of Gracie living on fast food or whatever inedible meals her father concocted.

She wasn't trying to worm her way into his good graces or to assuage the ravaged places in her own heart. If her rap on the burgundy front door was too loud, it was only because she wanted to get Xavier's attention. Not because guilt threatened to consume her.

Eight

Chapter 8

Xavier peered through the curtains for the twelfth time. Not that he was counting. Was she coming? Had the directions to his house been clear? He'd call her, except he didn't have her number. He should remedy that as soon as she showed up. If she showed up.

Because he hadn't been mistaken. Mackenzie disapproved of him. The distinct barrier she'd kept between them last night was enough to repel a fox. Yet, she'd been so soft and caring with Gracie that he'd have forgiven her for anything.

He peeked through the curtains again. He should have told her a definite time rather than suggesting she drop by around one. As it was, nap time was almost over and she still hadn't shown up. He swiped a hand down his face.

He was acting like a teenager on his first date. This wasn't a date. It was a rescue mission. The woman pitied Gracie and agreed to teach him the basic skills he should have already mastered.

He moved away from the window to pace in front of it. Four steps in one direction. Turn. Four steps back.

What if he created a game where the mentor character used cooking lessons to get their point across?

Xavier stopped in his tracks. Had he just had an idea for a game? It had been so long that he'd almost forgotten the rush of adrenaline he got with an idea. The zing in his chest when the idea had potential. He rubbed his chest. There had been a definite zing.

His eyes scanned the room for paper. He should jot down the idea before he forgot. Maybe he'd get enough ideas to sketch out the story. Someone pounded on the door.

"Coming." He hurried to open it before they woke Gracie. "Mackenzie."

He stepped back to let her in. "I should give you my number if we plan to do this again." He gestured to the door. "We don't want to wake Gracie."

She winced. "Sorry. I was distracted." She pulled off her coat. "Where should I put this?"

She glanced around the room while Xavier worked on not swallowing his tongue. Her purple dress hugged her lithe frame, and he sent up a quick prayer thanking God for sweater dresses.

"Uhm, I'll take it." He plucked it from her hand, his fingers brushing against hers. A thrill shot up his arm. There was definitely some emotional resurrection happening here.

Why her? The woman disliked him. Why was God allowing her to stir his emotions?

My thoughts are not your thoughts, nor are My ways your ways. The verse floated through his mind. Was God finally talking to him after His long silence?

He glanced at Mackenzie. "This way." He led her to the kitchen after placing her coat over the back of the couch. "We have about fifteen minutes before Gracie wakes up."

"Okay." She glanced around the kitchen. "Mind if I?" She gestured to the cupboards.

"No, go ahead." He leaned against the island in the center of the kitchen, tracking her movements with his eyes. She was light on her feet, a woman confident in herself, even in a strange room.

Maybe if he showed her how much he appreciated her help, she'd warm up to him. He shook his head. What was he doing? This wasn't about her. It was about Gracie. He should focus on learning to cook a basic meal for his child.

After she'd gone through each of his cupboards, she turned to him.

"Was there something in particular you wanted to learn how to cook?"

He'd thought about this. He'd done hours of internet research and collected dozens of recipes. Xavier had attempted a couple of them when Gracie had been at VBS, only to dump most of what he'd cooked into the trash.

"Rice." Since most of the recipes had rice as a side, he should start there. His efforts had either been too soggy or too hard. "And something chicken."

"Do you have a particular chicken recipe in mind?"

"No. Something easy to prepare and that Gracie won't mind eating every day until I learn to cook something else."

"Okay. Let's brown stew the chicken, as there are several ways to modify the recipe to add variety."

She slipped an apron over her head and Xavier allowed

himself a second to appreciate having her in his space.

Apparently, the trick to cooking rice was the ratio of water to rice. It was much simpler when Mackenzie explained it than in any cooking tutorial he'd read or watched. It turns out that you had to be precise with the proportions or disaster ensued.

Under Mackenzie's eagle eye, Xavier prepared the meal he prayed would be his first edible one.

"What are you doing?"

Xavier turned at Gracie's voice. "Mackenzie is teaching me how to cook."

Gracie wrinkled her nose. "I don't know about that, Daddy. You should stick to your strengths."

He snorted. "What would that be?" At the moment, he was batting zero when it came to things he did well.

"Making video games, silly." She came into the room and hugged Mackenzie's legs. "Daddy makes the best video games. All about God and the Bible and stuff."

"Sounds interesting." Mackenzie's complete focus had shifted to Gracie.

He shouldn't be jealous. He should be happy Gracie had a woman unrelated to her by blood taking an interest in her. Unfortunately, what we should do and what we did were often unrelated.

"Why are you looking at her that way, Daddy?"

Why did Gracie always catch him staring at Mackenzie? He shifted his attention to his cooking, stirring the chicken that didn't need stirring.

"How was your dad looking at me?"

"As if you're the—"

"Alana Grace." He may have shouted. His mind flashed to the conversation they'd had the day she'd been watching It Takes

Two. The last thing he wanted was for her to give Mackenzie the impression he was interested in her. Even if he was against his better judgment.

"I'm sorry, Daddy. Sometimes it's hard to keep my inside thoughts inside."

Mackenzie's gaze brimmed with curiosity, but he pretended not to notice.

"Can I show Miss M'kenzie the game, Daddy?"

And leave him alone in this kitchen? Mackenzie must have read his mind.

"You'll be fine." She opened the pot and took out a forkful of rice that had come out perfectly. "The rice is ready." She turned the flame off.

"As for the chicken, you have until the water dries out." She adjusted the flame under the pot. "If you're not sure what to do, come find me. I'll be with Gracie."

Mackenzie took Gracie's hand and followed her out of the kitchen. Why did he sense she was more interested in his daughter than in him?

He made to follow, but the desire to prepare one edible meal held him back. He'd stay in the kitchen, but he intended to find out everything about Mackenzie Porter because something wasn't quite right.

Nine

Chapter 9

Madison took her time studying the living room, now that she didn't have to contend with Xavier watching her. Brown and beige dominated the space. Someone had thrown blankets in blue and yellow over the back of the couches. The pops of color made the room inviting instead of boring.

"Do you like it, Miss M'kenzie?"

Madison shifted her attention to the child, her heart softening. "Yes."

"Daddy chose the yellow flowers because it's my favorite."

"Excellent choice."

"Let's play my favorite game."

Gracie turned on the television and the game console with the expert motions of someone who'd been doing it forever. Just how many hours did the child spend playing video games? She glared over her shoulder.

Get the full picture before you form an opinion.

Madison huffed out a breath. If only there was a way to mute her inner voice. But since it had been on track the last time she'd jumped to conclusions, she'd find out more before she labeled Xavier as a negligent parent.

"Why do you enjoy playing this game?"

The characters, though animated, were surprisingly lifelike.

"Because I get to be a queen." She handed Madison a console. "I'll set it so we can both play."

Madison tuned in to the narrator's voice. "Is this the story of Queen Esther?"

"Uh-huh. Did you know some guy wanted to kill her and all her people because he hated them?"

She nodded.

"Daddy says God protected His people then, the same way He protects us now."

Madison gaped at Gracie. Oh, to have such childlike faith, believing that God was good all the time. When had Madison started believing God was out to get her?

Was it while she'd been attending school in Italy? It had been the first time she'd been away from home and her longest separation from Mackenzie. She'd craved the adventure but had felt alone. Isolated.

After Sergio had broken her heart, God had deserted her too.

She shook her head. This was not the time to get maudlin. Without Xavier or anyone else in the room, she could probe into Gracie's life.

"What's your dad like? Does he spend lots of time with you?"

"Uh-huh." The little girl's eyes remained fixed on the screen. "He plays video games with me." Gracie's shoulders jerked as her character jumped to collect tokens. "Since Aunt Jacqui left, sometimes he reads stories to me. He's not a good cook."

What was she doing? This wasn't her. This person interrogating a child to find out what? That her father hurt her? It was obvious that Xavier cared about Gracie, even if he was helpless in the kitchen.

He loved his daughter and was doing his best to ensure she had a bright future. Instead of tearing him down, she should give him the tools to build their family up. It was the least she could do for Gracie.

She leaned her head closer to the child, inhaling her sweet strawberry scent. "Your daddy's trying real hard to learn. Why don't we go check on him?"

Madison stood and offered her hand to the child.

"Okay." Gracie paused the game and took her hand. "I was failing this level, anyway."

Madison chuckled as they headed back to the kitchen.

* * *

The smell of burnt meat had her rushing to the stove. "What are you doing?"

Xavier's head snapped up from where he sat at the kitchen counter, scribbling on a piece of paper.

She snapped off the burner and whirled on him, hands propped on her hips. "You had one thing to do. One thing," she ignored his sheepish expression and held up a finger. "That couldn't have waited until the chicken was done?"

"Uh-oh, Daddy, you're in trouble."

"Go to the living room, Gracie." Madison used her sternest voice, the one she'd perfected after only two days of VBS.

"Yes, Miss M'kenzie."

She resisted the twinge of guilt at the child's subdued tone, tracking her progress out of the room to ensure compliance. As soon as the door stopped swinging, she turned back to Xavier.

"Well?"

He massaged the back of his neck. "I had this idea for a game."

Her eyebrows shot up. This was about a stupid video game? Just when she'd convinced herself he wanted what was best for his daughter.

He winced. "You don't understand how momentous that was."

She tapped her feet, using the rhythm to temper her anger.

"I'm a video game designer."

"Really?" She drew the word out.

Xavier took a deep breath and exhaled, his shoulders heaving with the movement. "I'm a video game designer who hasn't designed a game in three years."

She stole a glance at the partition door before stepping closer to him. "Three years?"

"Not since my wife died. I haven't had a single idea since then. Until today. I had an idea before you came, but didn't get to write it down. I decided to do that while the chicken was cooking. Guess I got distracted. Sorry."

Madison's mind whirred as she processed what he'd told her.

"This move to Orange Valley—"

"Was also a way to jump-start my creativity. I have a lot riding on this move. I need to show my agent something in two months or he'll drop me as a client."

She needed time to process. Madison grabbed a bowl and began removing the pieces of the chicken that hadn't burned.

"Mackenzie," Xavier touched her hand.

"We can salvage some of this." She grabbed a different pot

and caught some water at the sink.

Xavier sighed. "Why am I telling you this when you hate me?"

She flicked him a glance. "I don't hate you."

He smirked. "No? Then why do you turn that disapproving glare on me all the time?"

"What disapproving glare?"

"That one." He pointed to her forehead, and she concentrated on smoothing her brow.

"I—" How'd she explain the myriad of emotions she felt around him?

Something about the sorrow in his eyes and the way he still cared about his wife years after her death endeared him to her. Or maybe it was his connection to Gracie that drew her to him.

At the same time, she resented him for not realizing the treasure Gracie was. Parenthood was a gift—one she wasn't sure he truly appreciated.

"Why'd you accept my help if you believed I hated you?"

"Forget it. I'll find someone else to help me figure this out." He massaged his forehead with two fingers. "I thought." He closed his eyes for a second. "Thanks for your help today, Mackenzie. I appreciate everything you taught me."

In an instant, Xavier had transformed from the approachable man she'd gotten used to into a distant stranger.

No. Her heart mourned the loss even as her brain processed what had happened.

"I'm sorry." She gave into her impulse and grabbed him. Heat shot up her arm, and Xavier hissed out a breath. She snatched her hand back. "Let me help you and Gracie. I'll do better."

Xavier sighed. "Can you at least tell me what you disapprove of?"

"I…"

Did she want to do this? Madison examined her motives. Everything she'd done up to this point had been to get close to Gracie. She'd used Xavier, impersonated her sister, and pretended to be someone she was not.

The trouble was that Xavier intrigued her. She wanted to uncover what lay beneath the surface. Because the only way she could release Gracie along with her dreams of motherhood into his hands was if she was sure he was a good parent.

Since she loved Gracie, she owed it to the little girl to help her father become the best dad he could be.

"You're not being a good parent." She sighed. "You're feeding her a steady diet of junk food. Then, you stick her in front of a screen when what she needs is time with you."

Xavier's eyes blazed. "Don't you think I know that? One reason I moved to Orange Valley was to take a shot at becoming the father she deserves."

He really believed that.

"Was it though? Because it sounds as though you'd failed at your video game career and rather than pivoting and trying something new, you ran away."

"What do you know about being a parent?"

She flinched.

"Nothing, and even I can tell what a shoddy job you're doing. You took Gracie away from a stable support system and brought her to a place where she's floundering."

She flung out an arm. "*You're* floundering. You didn't come to Orange Valley for Gracie. It was for Xavier—Xavier whose creativity had dried up and was afraid of becoming a has-been."

His shoulders sagged, the fire draining out of him. "You're right."

Ten

Chapter 10

Mackenzie blinked at him. "Excuse me?"

Xavier scraped a hand down his face. "You're right." He fumbled to sit on a stool before his legs failed him.

He plopped his head into his hands. He shouldn't have moved to Orange Valley. The whole time he'd convinced himself he was doing the best for Gracie, he'd been a selfish pig.

"Hey," her vanilla fragrance teased at his senses as she sat beside him.

He turned. "I'm sorry about what I said. About you not being a mother."

"It's the truth."

Maybe, but one that pained her. What was the story there? And why was he so concerned about this woman who admitted she disliked him and disapproved of his parenting style?

"You can become a better parent."

He snorted. What did she think this entire debacle had been about?

"You can." She rested a hand on his arm and he wanted more.

More than the meager slices of happiness he'd allowed himself for the last three years. He wanted more joy, more peace, more everything.

Because as much as he'd wished he had been the one to die, he was alive. Alarmingly so if his response to this woman was anything to go by. He wanted to live. To find someone to spend the rest of his life with.

He missed being one half of a partnership and might finally be ready to date again. But maybe he should try the dating thing with someone who found him attractive—after he got his parenting skills up to par.

He slipped his hand from under hers and ignored the hurt that flashed across her face. "Any ideas how I can do that? Cause you were it for me."

"Maybe we can do it together?" Her cautiously optimistic expression sparked his curiosity.

"What's in it for you?" He'd expected people to be nice, but this was too much. "Is this one of those cases where you get close to me and then kidnap my child?"

"What? No." She shook her head. "I would never hurt Gracie."

The genuine distress on her face did more to convince him than anything she said.

"Okay." He needed all the help he could get. "What do we do first?"

"Maybe focus on becoming the father Gracie needs you to be and less on the father you believe you should be."

* * *

Focus on becoming the father Gracie needs. Mackenzie's words became a mantra, thrumming through his head. How was he supposed to figure out what a five-year-old needed?

Xavier thought about his own father. Carl Washington had made mistakes, but Xavier could always count on him. He couldn't remember his father cooking a meal or washing an article of clothing, but he'd always been there.

Was it as straightforward as that? Was being a good father simply showing up for his daughter? Regardless of how he felt or how much he was struggling?

I will never leave you nor forsake you.

The words of his favorite verse washed over him, comforted him, and filled him with hope. As much as he wanted to cook a meal that didn't belong in a landfill, the thing he wanted most was for Gracie to know that he loved her and would always be there for her.

He'd checked out for the past few years…no, he wasn't going there. Hadn't he drawn a line in the sand to symbolize the change he was making in his parenting?

He wouldn't look back. He couldn't.

Xavier was the first parent at VBS. Usually, he waited in the main sanctuary for Gracie to come out to him. Today, he slipped into the Youth Department.

Children sat in clusters on floor cushions on the tiled floor. He scanned the room until he spotted Mackenzie's slender figure in the center of the cluster furthest from the door. She was completely at ease with the children. The remaining fear that she had nefarious ideas toward Gracie disappeared.

"Daddy!" Gracie disengaged herself from the group and

barreled toward him.

"Hey, Gracie-mine." He swung her up into his arms and approached Mackenzie.

"Ms. Porter."

She dipped her head in acknowledgment. There was a tiny dot of paint smudge beneath her ear. The urge to touch it was almost overwhelming.

He cleared his throat. "I'll just take Gracie's things and go."

He was still uncertain how to act around her after their last conversation.

"No, Daddy. I'm Miss M'kenzie's helper." She wriggled out of his arms. "I make sure no one leaves anything behind."

Which explains why she was always the last child out of the Youth Room.

Mackenzie smoothed a hand over Gracie's fuzzy hair. He needed to find a hairdresser soon.

"It's alright, sweetie. You can go with your dad."

"No-uh. Aunt Jacqui says when you make a promise, you keep it."

His five-year-old was already a better person than he was. He'd made promises—to Alicia. To himself. To Gracie. Promises he hadn't kept. God forgive him.

Lord, I don't know why I assumed I could do this by myself. I need You. Please help.

Eleven

Chapter 11

Madison drew the tasks out as long as she could. She folded and fluffed the floor cushions. She packed the supplies in the plastic tub for safekeeping, then checked and rechecked the area to see if the children had left anything behind.

Their last conversation left her uncertain of how to act in his presence. Her words and his were almost a physical thing between them.

"We got everything, Miss M'kenzie."

"Thanks, Gracie." She bent to hug the child. "I couldn't have done it without you." After she returned to Cinnamon Hill, there'd be no more hugs from Gracie. She cleared the emotion from her throat.

"Thanks for allowing her to stay back to help." She directed her words to a spot beyond Xavier's shoulder.

"Not a problem." He stepped closer. "You have a little…" He

brushed his fingers at a spot below her ear.

Madison hissed out a breath as shock pulsed through her at his touch. "What?"

"Paint."

"Oh." For a second, she'd hoped his touch would be for a more personal reason. She took a step back. Foolish. Why would Xavier have any interest in her? She'd told the man he was a horrible parent.

Besides, her only interest in him was as Gracie's father, wasn't it?

Gracie's eager face peered up at her. She'd missed whatever the child had said.

"I'm sorry. What was that?" She smoothed a hand over Gracie's hair.

"You should come with us, Miss M'kenzie." Gracie vibrated with excitement.

"No. You and your dad should spend time together."

"Daddy, you ask her." Gracie turned the force of her enthusiasm on Xavier.

"We're renting a Christmas tree. Apparently, that's what they do here in Orange Valley."

Madison nodded. Mackenzie had told her about the Christmas tree company that rented trees for the holidays. After the new year, they replanted the pines until the following Christmas.

"No, that's something for you and Daddy to do."

Gracie wrapped her arms around her legs. "I won't do it without you." Gracie peered up at her. "You're all alone for Christmas because you don't have a little girl. Since I don't have a mommy anymore, I'll be yours for the holiday. Daddy and I will be your Christmas family."

Madison's eyes flew to Xavier's. Somehow, the idea of being his for Christmas appealed to her. What would that entail? And why did she feel like she'd want to be his for a much longer time?

"I—" she swallowed hard. The sweetness of this child would be her undoing.

Lord, please help me.

The cry for help was sincere, though she wasn't sure what she preferred. Did she want God to get her out of going? Or to have Him convince Xavier to let her tag along?

Xavier's eyes rested on hers, curiosity and an emotion she couldn't identify swirling in their depths. Why was she attracted to the one man that was off-limits? Her gaze flicked down to Gracie. Because him being Gracie's father meant getting closer to him was a lousy idea.

* * *

Madison tucked her hands into the pockets of her coat, curling them into fists. She took a deep breath of the cool air, enjoying the scent of pines that filled her lungs. They'd outvoted her. She'd been no match for a persistent Gracie combined with Xavier's earnest expression. Why had he invited her to come along? Had it all been for Gracie?

She snuck a glance at him, trying to ignore the quiet strength he exuded. He caught her gaze and lifted a brow. Madison swiveled her head to scan the pine trees that stretched into the distance.

"How does this work? Do we just walk up to a tree and claim it? Or is there some kind of system?"

"There's a system, but we should go to the office first." Xavier spun in a slow circle. "I think we go that way." He pointed to a narrow opening between the trees. "According to the guy on the phone, the office is impossible to miss."

"Okay."

Gracie slipped her hand into her father's and Madison smiled. Her idea appeared to be working. A few steps in the direction Xavier had indicated, and Madison laughed out loud.

A bright red cottage with white trimmings sat at the beginning of a path that led into the trees. The design would have made the elves at the North Pole proud.

"Miss M'kenzie, it's Santa's house." Gracie brushed against Madison's side.

Madison beamed at the child. "Let's find the perfect tree."

Finding the ideal Christmas tree was easier than Madison had expected because the trees were all perfect. Each Christmas tree was in its own pot, waiting for its temporary owner to claim it.

Gracie affixed the large sticker on which Xavier had scrawled his first initial and surname to the pot of the tree they'd chosen. Then she leaned over and whispered.

"Don't worry, Mr. Tree, we'll take care of you."

Madison bit her cheek to hold back her smile. "Do we just take it now?"

"No. They'll deliver it to the house in the next couple of days. Something about keeping the environment ideal for the plant." Xavier shrugged. "The guy explained it, but I wasn't listening. I had other things on my mind."

The expression in his eyes raised her body temperature by at least ten degrees. Had he been thinking about her? Why did she want the answer to be yes?

His eyes dropped to her lips, and her mouth dried. Oh, my.

Heaven help her, but she craved his attention. She wanted his lips on hers. To know what he tasted like.

"Are you two going to kiss now?"

"What?" Her eyes snapped to Gracie. "No."

She'd forgotten about their mini chaperone. Madison stumbled back and would have crashed into one of the potted trees if Xavier hadn't grabbed her. "Why did you say that?"

Gracie jerked her shoulders. "You and Daddy were looking at each other like the people in—"

"Alana Grace." Xavier's voice held a touch of exasperation.

What people? Her eyes flitted between them.

"Did I do it again, Daddy?"

"Yes."

Gracie's shoulders sagged. "No wonder grown-ups are always sad. They have to keep all their words stuffed inside."

Madison and Xavier exchanged amused glances. The child had a point. Life would be simpler if people spoke freely. Then again, some people needed a filter.

"Gracie." Madison squatted and met her gaze. "I know you want to say all the words in your head, but sometimes, words hurt."

"Like when somebody's mean?"

"Yes. Sometimes you can hurt someone even when you weren't trying to be mean."

The girl's eyes widened. "I'm sorry, Miss M'kenzie. I'll keep some of my words in."

"I'm sure you'll do your best." She ran a hand over the girl's hair. Her twists were fuzzy and needed to be redone. Should she mention it? Or was there a way for her to have it taken care of?

"Can we get hot chocolate now? Daddy said I could get some

if I didn't get into any trouble." Gracie hopped over to her father. "I was good, wasn't I, Daddy?"

"You were." Xavier tapped her on the nose. "Let's go get hot chocolate." His lips quirked. "You should come too."

Madison resisted the urge to fan her face. Who needed hot chocolate when Xavier smiled at them like that? Ooh, boy, she was in trouble.

"Er–no. I have this thing to do. Rain check?"

Gracie wrinkled her nose. "What's a rain check?"

Madison focused all her attention on Gracie, anything to ignore Xavier and the havoc he was wreaking on her emotions. "It means the person can't do what you ask them to do that day, but they'll do it another time."

"Oh." Gracie's mouth turned down. "You can have your rain check, Miss M'kenzie."

"Yes. We know how busy you are." His smirk confirmed that he'd seen through her flimsy excuse.

"Yeah." Madison turned away from the appealing picture of Xavier and Gracie before her heart overrode her common sense.

Chapter 12

This is not a date. Xavier repeated the words as he checked and double-checked the chicken to ensure the gravy hadn't dried out. He'd discovered that a few spoonfuls of barbecue sauce changed the flavor of the dish.

"Not a date."

"Who are you talking to, Daddy?" Gracie had taken to sitting at the counter while he cooked. It was pretty much the same meal with slight variations, but neither of them had died yet.

"No one."

"If you say so." Her gaze dropped back to her coloring book.

This was not a date. Mackenzie was simply coming over at Gracie's insistence to help decorate the Christmas tree that had finally come.

It had taken him the better part of half a day to locate the decorations Alicia had collected during their marriage. Okay, it had taken half a day to drum up the courage to go into the attic and less than five minutes to locate the boxes once he'd gotten there.

Jacqui had done an excellent job of sorting and unpacking. All the boxes had a label listing their contents.

Guilt niggled at him. Should he call her? She and Gracie had had several conversations since she'd left, but he hadn't spoken to her except for a tense greeting before he handed the phone to Gracie.

Somehow, it didn't seem fair to Jacqui to navigate her emotions when his head was tangled up with someone else. There was a knock on the door, and he almost jumped a foot. Gracie giggled.

"You're so silly, Daddy. That's just Miss M'kenzie." She hopped from the stool and rushed out of the room.

"Don't open the door."

He twisted the burner off before following her. Gracie danced in front of the door as she waited for him to catch up. Xavier was as anxious as she was.

Mackenzie filled the dark places inside him with light. He wanted to bask in her sunshine—he snatched the door open to shut up his thoughts.

When had his inner voice gotten this fanciful, anyway? He'd become a lovesick teenager.

"Hi, Mackenzie." He stood back for her to enter. Something flickered in her eyes and he frowned. Had he upset her? Already? Her attention shifted to Gracie, and her entire face lit up.

"Hi, Gracie."

"Miss M'kenzie." Gracie flung herself into Mackenzie's arms and their mutual affection for each other stirred something inside. Envy? Xavier struggled to identify the emotion. Yes, but also longing. He wanted a place in her arms as well.

Was it possible to figure out the type of man Mackenzie wanted? To *become* the man she wanted? He shook his head to dispel the foolish notion.

"The tree is this way." His voice was more gruff than normal. He hurried to the living room before anyone commented.

Get ahold of yourself, man. This woman is not interested in you.

He took several deep breaths and was more himself by the time Mackenzie and Gracie entered the room.

Mackenzie surveyed the pile of decorations and smirked. "Did you have a few more trees you planned to decorate?"

Xavier rubbed the back of his neck. "We're used to a bigger tree."

This tree only came as high as his chest. If he stacked all the decorations, they'd be almost the same height as the tree.

"Okay. Maybe we should start with the decorations that are special to you. Is there anything you'd want on your tree?"

Not really. Since Alicia's death, he'd left the decorations to Jacqui or his mom…anyone willing to decorate the tree.

If it had been up to him, there'd have been no Christmas celebrations. But the women in his life had insisted Gracie needed the traditions—to remember the reason for the season. That she needed to celebrate, even when walking through grief.

"Can we use the Memory Line, Daddy?"

"Memory Line?" Mackenzie arched a brow.

"Yeah." It had been Alicia's idea. Xavier shifted through a few boxes before finding the ornament. "Here."

He handed the ornament to Mackenzie. Alicia had bought a pack of photo sleeves and punched a hole in one corner. She'd run a string through each hole, linking the sleeves together to create a chain. Some sleeves had photos, but most were empty.

"What's this?" Mackenzie had settled cross-legged on the floor, Gracie leaning against her.

"Our Memory Line." Gracie flipped to one of the earlier photos. "This is Mommy and Daddy."

Their wedding picture. He and Alicia beamed at the camera. They'd been so young, their whole lives ahead of them. Mackenzie touched Gracie's ultrasound. It had come with Gracie's adoption records, along with photos of her birth mother—always from the neck down or in profile, never showing her face.

"This is one of my favorites. It's a picture of me before I came out of my other Mommy's tummy."

"Gracie's adopted. We got the ultrasound with her adoption papers."

Mackenzie's lips quirked into a sad smile. "I bet both of your mommies loved you very much."

The black and white ultrasound was out of place among the photos, but Alicia had insisted it belonged there. He cleared his throat.

"Alicia believed we should acknowledge the gift we'd received, even if we never got to thank Gracie's birth mom in person."

Mackenzie's eyes filled, and a single tear spilled and ran down her cheek. Would it be too much if he wiped it away? If he caught the pearl of moisture with his thumb? His gaze shot to the ultrasound that she caressed with reverent fingers.

Say something. Anything.

"It's not too cheesy?"

She shook her head. "It's beautiful." Her voice was husky. "Gracie's birth mom would appreciate it."

"I hope so. Alicia and I agreed to raise Gracie with the knowledge that her birth mom had gifted her to us."

Tears were flowing from Mackenzie's eyes now. Maybe he should stop talking. This conversation was only upsetting her.

"What's the matter, Miss M'kenzie? Did you lose your mommy, too?" Gracie pressed up to her knees and used her tiny hands to dry Mackenzie's tears.

Xavier firmed his heart against the desire to drop beside Mackenzie and kiss her tears away.

"No, sweetie, but I understand how much your birth mommy would appreciate what your Mommy and Daddy have done."

Xavier's eyes snapped to her face. What did that mean? Had Mackenzie given up a child for adoption? Was that why she got along so well with Gracie? Because she reminded Mackenzie of her daughter? Except he hadn't mentioned Gracie's adoption status until today.

Thirteen

Chapter 13

She would have to tell him. Madison forked up some of her carrot salad. She had enjoyed the dish the other night and hoped it would cheer her up now. But she could have been eating a pile of broccoli for as much joy as it brought her.

He was going to hate her. Gracie would hate her. She wasn't sure which one of the two outcomes hurt worst.

"Mackenzie?" Someone touched her shoulder, and she jumped. "I'm sorry. Did I frighten you?"

She smiled at Brianna. "It's okay. I needed a break from my thoughts." She mock-shuddered. "Now those were scary. What's up?"

"I was supposed to meet a client, but she called and canceled." Brianna gestured to the chair across from her. "Mind if I join you?"

"Sure."

"You're glum." Brianna dropped into the seat. "Want to talk about it?"

Not really.

"Come on," Brianna wheedled. "It will help you feel better." She laughed. "Besides, you'll help me practice my pastor's wife's wisdom."

Madison raised an eyebrow. "Is that a thing?"

"The congregation believes it is. Some people believe the second I married Daniel, God endowed me with heavenly wisdom. My aim is to show them that acquiring godly wisdom is a process. One we all have access to if we develop our relationship with God."

That made sense—except she'd turned her back on God, and walked away from Him when she realized the family she dreamed of would never happen.

"Yes, well," she stuffed a forkful of salad into her mouth, as a delay tactic. She needed to tell someone what she was dealing with, but how could she? Everyone in Orange Valley believed she was Mackenzie.

You could tell Mackenzie.

She couldn't tell her sister. If she did, she'd have to admit she'd kept an enormous secret for six years. Her sister wouldn't forgive her for that, could she?

Brianna frowned. "Are you enjoying that?"

"Hmm-mph." She hurried to chew and swallow the mouthful. "I adore carrots and this salad is one of the best I've ever tasted."

It was creamier than she was used to. Maybe she could get the recipe from the chef.

"Don't you hate carrots?" Brianna cocked her head. "And what was it you liked?" She snapped her fingers. "Broccoli."

Madison's nose wrinkled. Ugh. Just the prospect of eating

the dwarf trees had a physical effect on her. "Eww."

"What's going on?" Brianna's brow wrinkled. "Mackenzie?"

Madison sighed. "Madison."

She was relieved to say her name aloud.

"Excuse me?" Brianna's laugh had a nervous edge.

"My name's Madison. Mackenzie is my twin."

Brianna's eyes widened as her mouth rounded into an oh. "I didn't know Mackenzie had a twin." Brianna leaned closer to peer at her. "You look exactly alike."

The corner of her lips quirked. "Not quite."

There were tiny differences between them, but most people never paid close enough attention to notice. She and Mackenzie had decided they wouldn't marry unless the guy could tell the two of them apart.

"So, Mac-Madison."

"Shh."

Brianna glanced around the restaurant, then lowered her voice. "Does Xavier know?"

"No."

"But I thought the two of you were getting closer."

"That's the problem." Madison plopped her face into her hands. She hadn't been able to sleep at all the night before. At VBS, she'd barely been able to function and had been happy when all the parents picked up their children so she could leave.

"You should tell him."

She lifted her head to glare at Brianna. "Why do you think I'm burying my sorrow in carrot salad?"

"Let's talk through it." Brianna grabbed her hands before Madison could cover her face again.

"What are you afraid will happen? At most, he'll be upset that you kept this from him. But he seems like a nice guy. He won't be angry for long."

Except that wasn't the biggest secret she was keeping from Xavier, was it?

Brianna regarded her with sympathy. The desire to come clean had the words bubbling up out of her mouth. Only years of practice and the sense of disloyalty to Mackenzie kept them locked inside.

Because, if anyone should hear *that* secret first, it should be her twin. Then her family. Xavier. Gracie. She groaned. Lots of people would be angry and hurt because of what she'd done.

"Madison?" Brianna's voice dragged her out of her thoughts.

"Please don't say anything until I decide what to do."

"Madison—"

"Please." She clutched Brianna's hands. She wanted to fix her house of cards before everything came tumbling down.

"Oh-kay." Brianna's expression could curdle milk. "What do I call you in the meantime? I won't feel right to call you Mackenzie when I know you're not her."

"Emmy." Her family's nickname for her rolled off the tongue.

"Emmy." Brianna smiled. "I like that."

So did she. It had been her idea to switch places with Mackenzie, but the comfort of someone knowing the truth about her identity was undeniable.

She could be Emmy. Maybe her confession to Xavier should start there—with a tiny lowering of the barrier she'd erected between them.

Chapter 14

Xavier saw Mackenzie everywhere. In his kitchen when he prepared a meal. In the living room, when he spent time with Gracie or relaxed. At church. He even saw her in his dreams.

This fascination that bordered on obsession with a woman who disliked him was ridiculous. Yet he couldn't shake the feeling that his and Mackenzie's lives were irretrievably intertwined. Must be wishful thinking.

"Are you ready to go, Gracie?"

"I'm ready, Daddy."

He grinned at his daughter, who'd dressed in Christmas colors in thick green tights and a green corduroy dress. He buttoned her red jacket all the way to the neck and pointed to her red boots.

"Do I look like Christmas, Daddy?"

Alicia should be here for this moment. Grief blindsided him

as it often did. He cleared his throat.

"You're perfect. I plan to hold your hand extra tight." He lowered his voice. "I don't want Santa's helpers to steal you away."

Her smile melted his heart.

"In fact," he whipped out his phone. "This picture will go on the Memory Line."

He captured several poses before Gracie danced with impatience.

"Come on, Daddy. We'll miss the tree lighting."

"Alright, alright." He chuckled. This was what he'd been missing out on all this time? His daughter was a treasure.

He held her hand as she skipped beside him toward the town square.

"Will Miss M'kenzie be there?"

Would she? Something inside him thrilled at the idea of seeing her again, of maybe chipping away a little of her resolve toward him.

"Maybe. But there will be lots of people there. We may not find her in the crowd."

No sense in the two of them pining for something that wouldn't happen.

"She'll find us." Gracie nodded with certainty.

Her words were confident. Did she have an insight into the inner workings of Mackenzie's mind?

"Maybe."

Gracie stopped walking, forcing him to do the same.

"We'll see Miss M'kenzie today."

She truly believed that.

"How do you know?"

Gracie shuffled her feet, following the movement with her

eyes. A scene from the movie flashed through his mind. Was his daughter playing matchmaker?

"Alana Grace? Did you do something so that Ms. Mackenzie would find us?"

"No."

She still refused to meet his gaze. He squatted and waited until she did.

"I just do. When I'm with Miss M'kenzie, I feel like my heart's attached to hers." Her voice dropped to a whisper. "Sometimes, I think the same thing happens to her."

A shiver worked its way down his spine. Did he believe her? Xavier scrutinized her. What choice did he have? Gracie never lied to him. Her unfailing honesty was the reason he had to curtail her words.

They resumed their walk into the square, but even the increasing press of the crowd couldn't distract him from Gracie's odd statement.

"What happened to all the lights, Daddy?" Gracie tugged on his arm.

The closer they got to the square, the darker the storefronts became. There was enough light to see, and a powerful light source drew attention to the Christmas tree.

"Someone turned them off, so we'd focus on the Christmas tree."

"Oh."

As he'd expected, the square was crowded. He allowed his eyes to adjust to the lighting before scanning the gathering for Mackenzie's familiar frame. Did he really believe his five-year-old daughter and the woman he was mooning over had a heart connection? Gracie tugged on his coat.

"I can't see, Daddy."

Right. He had a more important bond to strengthen. He lifted Gracie into his arms and pressed toward the front of the crowd.

The majestic tree towered over them, a giant lever a few feet away. How many hours had it taken to decorate that massive tree? The mayor, a matronly woman who resembled someone's grandmother, took the stage.

"As much as I know you all braved the cold to see me this evening, I won't keep you long."

The crowd tittered, and Xavier grinned. He was glad the mayor didn't take herself too seriously.

"First, please remember the fundraiser being held by Morningside Hospital on Boxing Day. Proceeds are in aid of medical care for several patients in need of surgery. Tickets are available at Ruby's Place, The Fair Child, or at Morningside."

Xavier made a mental note to buy a couple of tickets, even if they didn't attend.

"Now," the mayor clapped her hands, "the moment we've all been waiting for. We can spend the next twelve months debating whether Jesus was born in December. Or we can argue about whether it's right to use a symbol that began in paganism to celebrate His birth.

"Or we can spend this time giving thanks to our Creator because He saw the immense need humanity had for a Savior and answered it.

"Whether you choose to accept Jesus as your Lord and Savior or not, He died for your sins because He loves you. Let's not get so caught up in gifts and revelry that we forget about Him."

"Daddy," Gracie whisper-shouted close to his ear. "What's rev-revel- that word?"

"Parties and having fun."

"Oh, we don't do that."

No, but wallowing in grief and pain didn't honor the Creator, either. There was a time for mourning, yes, but didn't God say joy comes in the morning?

He'd been extending his night and period of mourning as though it was a badge of honor when it was a sign of *dishonor*. It was a lack of appreciation for the air that coursed through his lungs, the family he still had, and the purpose God had given him.

So maybe he no longer had ideas for video games, but couldn't God create beauty from ashes? Couldn't God breathe life into something that was dead?

Take his relationship with Gracie—he'd feared that it had been irreparably damaged because he'd neglected her in his grief. After a few days of trying harder, his daughter reached for him more often. She sought him out for comfort, and together they were creating a new life in Orange Valley.

"Without further ado," the mayor continued. "Let's light this place up."

Someone turned off the light that highlighted the tree. For a second, there was only darkness, and then the tree flickered to life, as did the storefronts of the buildings closest to the square.

Gracie gasped, joining in the applause as the citizens celebrated. Across the crowded square, his eyes met Mackenzie's.

Fifteen

Chapter 15

Madison's eyes connected with Xavier's and something sparked to life inside her. She hadn't planned on attending the tree lighting, but sitting in Mackenzie's house being pummeled by guilt was less appealing.

Her eyes shifted to Gracie, who clapped with enthusiasm from within the curve of her father's arms. She wanted that—to be part of their inner circle. How would she tell him what she'd done? That she'd lied to him?

He'd hate her. Wouldn't it be better for her to fix their relationship before she dumped her confessions on him? Yes, she angled her chin, shoring up her resolve.

She'd treat him the same as any other man she'd just met. She'd extend grace about him not being the best father. He'd already improved since she'd said those harsh words to him.

Yes. She'd show him they didn't have to be enemies, and when she made her big confession, he'd be willing to forgive her.

Her feet were in motion before her head had built an argument against what it was convinced was a stupid idea.

"Miss M'kenzie!" Gracie almost leaped out of her father's arms. "Told you, Daddy."

"Hey, Gracie." She swiped a hand over the girl's hair, enjoying the brief contact. "Xavier."

She forced herself to meet his gaze. In the faux daylight of the Christmas lights, she glimpsed amazement and…Fear? She took a step back. Had he guessed her secret?

"E-everything alright?"

"I believe my daughter has the gift of prophecy."

"What?" She chuckled to hide her discomfort.

"I told him you'd be here, Miss M'kenzie, and that you'd find us." Gracie wriggled until her father set her on her feet. "We're having hot chocolate and then we'll watch Christmas movies. You should come with us."

Gracie grabbed her hand.

"No."

The crowd had dispersed after the tree lighting as people moved on to other activities. Madison stepped back. She was supposed to be nicer to the man, not plant herself in the middle of his outing with his daughter.

"Miss M'kenzie, you promised."

Her eyes dropped to Gracie.

"You said we'd be your Christmas family. Well, families have hot chocolate together when it's cold."

Madison nibbled her bottom lip. She hadn't exactly agreed to Gracie's temporary adoption, but she hadn't resisted, either.

"Besides, we have to give you back your rain check."

Was the child as hungry for a maternal figure as Madison

was for a child to fill her arms?

Nothing good will come from this.

"My daddy makes the best hot chocolate."

The man who couldn't cook? Madison wasn't holding her breath. "We'll see."

She wouldn't be the one to dull the shine of Gracie's faith in her father's hot chocolate-making capabilities.

"Hot chocolate you said?" She reached for Gracie's hand, beaming when the girl clutched hers. "Hot chocolate is my favorite Christmas drink, apart from sorrel and eggnog."

Gracie giggled. "You have a lot of favorites, Miss M'kenzie."

Madison wrinkled her nose. Wasn't she also supposed to be reclaiming her identity?

"Why don't you call me Emmy?"

Gracie swung their joint hands and peered up at her. "Miss Emmy sounds weird."

Madison chuckled. "So it does. Just Emmy."

Gracie gasped. "I can't. Aunt Jacqui says I'm not to call grown-ups anything except Miss or Mister."

This Jacqui had a lot of influence on Gracie. Was there more to the relationship between Jacqui and Xavier than she'd assumed? The thought twisted her gut.

Xavier squatted down to meet Gracie's eyes. "Aunt Jacqui said that to remind you to be respectful of grown-ups." His gaze flickered to hers.

"Since Miss Mackenzie—"

"Emmy."

Xavier held her gaze. "Emmy."

Her nickname had never sounded as good as it did in his low, rumbly voice.

"Since Emmy gave you permission to call her that, it will be okay."

"Well," Gracie twisted her foot from side to side. "I guess it's okay. But only when we're not at VBS. I don't want the others to feel bad."

Alana Grace was the sweetest child she'd ever met. Was it any wonder Madison had fallen in love with her?

* * *

Gracie had been right. Madison wasn't sure what she'd expected from the man who'd never cooked for himself until about two weeks ago. Certainly nothing more than him tearing open a packet and adding it to a cup of hot water. Maybe a few pieces of semi-sweet chocolate the way her mom did, or a handful of mini marshmallows like her dad.

She hadn't expected a full-on cocoa bomb about the size of a baseball. Oh, it wasn't as pretty as some she'd seen online but promised to throw a chocolate punch unlike anything she'd had before.

"What's in it?"

"You'll love it, Miss—Emmy." The little girl vibrated with excitement. "It has lots and lots of chocolate and marshmallows. Daddy crams it in there and it explodes when it melts in your cup."

Madison switched her gaze between the chocolate balls that sat nestled in a plastic container and Xavier.

"You made these?" She still couldn't believe it.

Xavier looked up from the pot of milk he was heating on the stove. "Uh-huh."

"I thought you couldn't cook?" Her tone may have been a tad accusatory.

One corner of Xavier's mouth lifted. "I'm not sure anyone would consider making a chocolate bomb cooking."

She would. She and Mackenzie had learned to cook when they were Gracie's age, yet the video tutorials had intimidated her too much for her to try.

Xavier snapped the burner off and filled three teacups three-quarters full. "That way, it doesn't spill over as the chocolate melts." He explained without turning to her.

"I'll go set up the movie, Daddy." Gracie skipped out of the room.

Madison shook her head, marveling that Xavier Washington made chocolate bombs. "You're full of surprises."   .

"You still hate me." Xavier used tongs to remove three balls from the container and put them in a small bowl that he set on a tray.

She caught her breath at his murmured words. "I don't hate you." Exactly.

"Really?" His eyebrows shot up. "Because I know precisely how much you care about Gracie. Every time you look at my daughter, your face lights up."

She took a step back at the fierce light in his eyes.

"G-Gracie's easy to love."

"She is." Xavier agreed, taking a step toward her. "What I can't figure out is why you get a line on your forehead every time you look at me."

"A-a line?" Madison concentrated on relaxing her face.

Xavier narrowed the gap between them.

"I don't get a line on my forehead." She stepped backward, closing her eyes when her back pressed against the island. She had nowhere to go unless she pushed him away.

What was she thinking? She was a grown woman. And

as much as Xavier had literally backed her into a corner, she wasn't afraid of him.

"Sure you do. It's right here." He closed the gap between them. He ran his forefinger across her brow and Madison drew in a breath as heat sizzled across her skin.

"Why does it matter?" She willed her voice to be forceful, a lion facing down a cheetah. Instead, it came out as a breath.

"Because Emmy. " He reached an arm behind her. "Maybe I desire some of that attention for myself."

Xavier snatched a handful of napkins and stepped back. Madison blinked. Had that been his goal all along? She swallowed. She'd truly thought…no, why would Xavier kiss her? He assumed she hated him.

Maybe she had resented him in the beginning. Now, her only concern was how she could attract some of his attention for herself.

Sixteen

Chapter 16

H e was out of his mind. What else could explain the scene he'd just enacted in the kitchen?

In the three years since he'd been a widower, he'd never had a flicker of interest for another woman. And considering that Jacqui had practically auditioned to become a sister-wife, that was saying a lot.

He smothered a wince. He had no right to make light of Jacqui's feelings. Especially since he now found himself in a similar situation—longing for someone who had no desire to get to know him better.

Why did moving to Orange Valley make him crave female companionship when he'd been fine all along?

He cast a glance at Mackenzie. She'd tucked herself at the end of the couch, keeping Gracie between them as a shield. Maybe he should start dating again.

She took a sip of her hot chocolate and moaned, her eyes

drifting shut. Good thing Gracie was there to chaperone. Best to think about something else.

"How is it?" He tipped his chin at her.

"It's good." She kept her eyes lowered, blowing on the liquid in her cup.

"I'd say it's more than good." He smirked. "I thought you were having a religious experience."

Her lips twitched. "Okay. It's more than good." She wiped a drop of chocolate from the corner of her mouth and sucked it off her finger.

He stared at the moving images on the screen. If someone asked him what the movie was about for a million dollars, he wouldn't have a clue.

Better to marry than to burn.

Yeah. He acknowledged the truth of the verse. The next time he went to church or picked up Gracie, he'd talk to one of the single women who were always staring at him. From there, he'd ease into dating. Then he'd get Mackenzie out of his system. Either that, or he'd fall in love for real.

* * *

Xavier sat in his office re-reading the story he'd written so far for what he hoped would be his new video game. When the phone rang, he scowled. Especially after he glimpsed the caller ID.

He didn't want to answer, didn't want to replay another version of the same conversation he'd been having with his agent for two long years.

But if he didn't answer, Noah would show up at his door. No doubt someone in his family had already given Noah his address.

Besides, before Alicia's death, he'd considered Noah Rodriguez a friend. The man had taken him on when designing video games had only been a dream. Noah had fought for him when no one had known his name.

"Hello."

"I was about to drive to Orange Valley for us to have this conversation."

Noah got to the point. One reason Xavier respected him. He offered his friend the courtesy of honesty.

"That's the only reason I answered."

Noah sighed. "I guess that means the move changed nothing."

His friend's disappointment thrummed between them.

"I did have an idea."

"Yeah?"

Xavier imagined his friend leaning forward as he usually did when he was excited.

"Will it pan out?"

"Maybe." He'd been writing the story at night after Gracie went to bed, but something about the gameplay concerned him.

"Tell me about it."

Xavier outlined the concept he'd come up with. "The thing I can't figure out is how to draw the avatar into the story."

"What if the mentor is the narrator?"

Xavier sat up. "Yes, and as she's telling the story, the characters act it out. Noah, you're a genius."

"I keep telling you that."

"Yeah, yeah. Gotta go." His fingers flew over the keypad as he blended Noah's idea with his into a new storyline.

Minutes melded into hours until someone banged on his

door. Xavier dragged himself out of the story and stumbled to the front door.

"Alright, I'm coming." He shouted at whoever it was, hoping they wouldn't break down his door before he got to it. He peeked through the side window.

Gracie and Mackenzie stood outside. He jerked the door open, heart racing.

"Everything alright?"

Mackenzie's eyebrow quirked. "That's what we wanted to ask you."

"Why isn't Gracie at VBS?" His eyes dropped to his daughter, checking for visible signs she'd been hurt. Tears shimmered in her eyes and her lips were pressed into a line.

"Honey?" He dropped onto his haunches.

Gracie folded her arms across her chest. "You forgot about me, Daddy. VBS ended hours and hours ago."

Oh, no. He lifted horrified eyes to Mackenzie. How had he forgotten about his precious girl? And why did he constantly do the worst things in this woman's presence?

If she told anyone about his behavior, he could say goodbye to any feeble inclination he had to date again.

"I figured you had a reason." Mackenzie lifted the other brow. "One that you'll share with us. Inside."

"Oh." Xavier stumbled to his feet and held the door for them.

"Well, Daddy?" Gracie tapped her foot. "Why did you forget about me?"

He massaged the back of his neck. "I didn't forget about you, honey." He grimaced, struggling for truth that wouldn't be damaging. "I got caught up in a game."

Gracie pouted. "Playing video games is not a good reason."

He tweaked her nose. "I wasn't playing games, Gracie-mine.

I was writing one."

Her lips rounded into an oh. "That's wonderful, Daddy."

"Uh-huh." He swung her into his arms and twirled around the room until she giggled.

"Xavier, that's amazing." Mackenzie's voice had the impact of a stop sign. He'd forgotten she was there.

"Yes." His eyes met hers.

"Is this the first one since?" Her eyes dropped to Gracie.

"Yes." He swallowed. "The one you inspired."

"Oh, my." Her hand fluttered to her throat. "I've never been someone's muse before."

"Well, you are now."

She laughed, the sound reminding him of tinkling bells. "What are you doing? Put Gracie down." She made a shooing motion. "Gracie, go put your stuff in your room. Your dad has a video game to write."

Gracie rushed off to do as Mackenzie said without a word of complaint.

"I should start dinner."

"No, you shouldn't." She grabbed his arms. "You have work to do."

Her sweet vanilla scent wrapped around him, and he wanted nothing more than to bury his nose in her neck and fill his lungs with her scent.

"Emmy." His hands settled on her waist as if it was the most natural thing in the world.

"Yes?"

Her tongue darted out to moisten her lips, and his eyes followed the motion. His grip tightened, drawing her closer. He couldn't date another woman. It was Mackenzie he wanted. But how was he supposed to convince her to take a chance on him?

Seventeen

Chapter 17

Madison sent Gracie to call her father for dinner. She didn't want to share a secluded space with Xavier. Otherwise, she'd claim the kiss she was sure he'd been about to deliver earlier.

If Gracie's footsteps hadn't announced her approach, she was pretty sure Xavier would've kissed her. And she'd wanted him to, had wanted his lips on hers and to be the focus of all his attention.

"Something smells good."

Madison jerked, the fork she'd been using to stir the pasta clattering to the floor. Gracie pounced on the fork before she could move.

"It's just spaghetti and meatballs." She met his gaze. Mistake. The heat in his eyes warmed her from the inside out. "I-I cooked dinner for you and Gracie." She reached to untie the apron strings. "I'll leave now so you can eat."

"No." He was before her in an instant, standing close enough for her to get a whiff of his spicy cologne when she inhaled.

"Stay for dinner. Wouldn't that be nice, Gracie?" He spoke without taking his eyes off hers.

"Yes! Please stay, Emmy."

How was a girl supposed to resist such an offer?

"Okay." She swallowed, though her mouth had gone dry. "I'll stay for dinner."

"Good."

The hum of attraction she had for Xavier turned into a roar—one she feared would devour her before she figured out what to do with it.

***

Madison jerked awake. Her arm had gone numb. Where was she? Her eyes roamed around the unfamiliar bedroom, its wall the palest shade of yellow. Someone moaned and her eyes dropped to the numb arm. Gracie.

Images from the night before came rushing back. She'd had dinner with Xavier and Gracie. They'd watched a movie before Xavier had disappeared into his office.

Gracie had begged her for a bedtime story. She must have fallen asleep. Why hadn't Xavier woken her up? The idea of a walk of shame was not appealing. She lay there for a few more minutes, trying to determine how to get out of her current predicament.

If Mackenzie was here...but her twin sister wasn't here. Madison would have to figure this out by herself. If anyone asked, she'd been taking care of Gracie.

She wriggled from under Gracie's arm to answer the call of

nature, snagging her phone on her way to the bathroom. She did her business before using some of Gracie's toothpaste on her finger to freshen her breath.

Madison sat on the edge of the bathtub and swiped at her phone. Fifteen missed calls. She frowned. What on earth was going on? She scrolled through her call log. Several of her friends had called, even some who were more frenemies than friends.

One of them had sent the link to a video. Madison pulled it up. Her mouth dropped open. Well, no wonder her phone was blowing up. And just who was she supposed to be kissing in Cinnamon Hill when she'd been in Orange Valley all this time?

"Emmy?"

"Yes, sweetie?"

"Good, you're still here." The relief in the little girl's voice made her smile. She returned to the bedroom to find Gracie sitting up in bed.

"Can I have something to eat? I'm hungry."

Madison nibbled at her bottom lip. The longer she stayed here, the more likely someone would catch her coming out of Xavier's house and draw the wrong conclusions.

"Please?" Gracie clasped her hands beneath her chin and pleaded with her eyes.

"Alright. After you eat breakfast, I'll take you to the park."

She'd make a detour to Mackenzie's house for a shower and a change of clothes. Yesterday had been the last day of VBS, so she'd take care of Gracie, giving Xavier time to write.

"What time does your father normally wake up?"

Gracie shrugged. "I don't know."

"Okay." She went over to kiss the child on the forehead. "Why don't you make your bed and get ready? Come downstairs when you're done."

She found Xavier in his office, wearing yesterday's clothes. He'd fallen asleep in one of the gaming chairs. Since she didn't have the heart to wake him, she tiptoed out of the room and went to make breakfast.

* * *

Alana Grace was the slowest breakfast eater in the world. Had she eaten this slowly last night?

"I hate this thing, Emmy." Gracie poked at the braised liver Madison had cooked to go with the boiled bananas.

Ah.

"Liver's good for you." Her mother's response popped out of her mouth before she could censor it.

Gracie's nose wrinkled. "Tastes yucky."

"Alright." Madison stood, reaching for Gracie's plate. "Guess we won't go to the park today."

"No." Gracie held up her hands to block Madison from taking her plate. The child drew in a deep breath. "I'll eat it, won't let this stinky liver win."

Madison bit back a smile. "I'll clean up the kitchen." And sneak in a call to her sister. "Can I trust you to eat everything before I come back?"

"I promise, Emmy."

She studied the girl's face. In the two weeks since Madison had known her, Gracie had never lied to her. Her conscience pricked her to tell the whole truth, but she pressed it to the back of her mind. Soon. She'd confess everything soon.

"Okay. I'll be back." She ducked into the kitchen and dialed her sister's number. When Mackenzie answered, she got to the point.

"Why am I on the evening news kissing a guy on the Mistletoe Cam? And why is everybody in Cinnamon Hill calling to ask me about my mystery man? Who is the mystery man?"

Mackenzie groaned. "What time is it?"

Madison frowned. "Are you still sleeping?"

"Can't talk, Emmy. I have to go. I'm late."

Late for what? Had Mackenzie forgotten the store was closed for the rest of the year? Maybe. It had been a while since Mackenzie had worked at their family's antique shop.

Madison tapped her phone to switch to a video call. "Are you okay?"

Madison pressed her face closer to the screen.

"Of course." Mackenzie feigned innocence. "I'm fine."

Nice try, Mackenzie, but Madison knew all about pretending.

"Did you forget what day it is?"

"Uhm."

"It's the twenty-third." Madison supplied. "The day of the auction. Did you forget?"

"What time is it again?"

Madison's frown deepened. It was in the appointment book at the shop. Something was seriously up with her sister.

"2:30."

A smile crept over Mackenzie's face.

"What is going on with you?" Madison arched a brow. "You're glowing."

"I am not!"

She was. Her sister appeared to be lit up from the inside.

"I'm still waiting for you to answer my questions. Who were you kissing at the basketball game?"

Mackenzie's eyes widened. "How do you know about that?"

Madison smirked at her. "It made the news."

Gracie came into the kitchen, cradling her empty plate.

"Emmy, I wanna go to the park. You said we could go if I ate my breakfast."

A soft smile crept across Madison's face. Gracie slid her plate into the sink. Gracie was such a sweetheart.

"Whose child is that?" Mackenzie squinted at the screen. "Where are you? Did you paint my kitchen?"

Madison whipped her head around. "What?" Paint her kitchen? "No! Why would I do that?"

Mackenzie pointed at the wall beyond Madison's shoulder. "Then why is my kitchen the wrong color? Who is the child in the background? Where are you?"

How had she forgotten Mackenzie's kitchen was yellow? She was tired of keeping secrets. Her eyes dropped to Gracie, who was trying to peek at her screen.

If Gracie saw Mackenzie or vice versa, she'd have a lot of explaining to do. Explanations she needed to make, but not now.

"I have to go."

Before Mackenzie said another word, she disconnected the call.

She took Gracie's hand. "What do you say we go to the park?"

When Mackenzie called her back, Madison pressed the reject button.

Chapter 18

When Xavier stumbled out of his office, the house was silent. After he'd tucked Gracie in last night, she'd demanded Emmy read her a story. Mackenzie had sat on the bed at his daughter's insistence, stroking the little girl's hair. Seeing them together had stirred up a longing inside him.

He wanted Mackenzie to be a permanent part of his household. And not as a caretaker for his daughter. While she'd read to Gracie, he'd snuck off to his office to write for another twenty minutes or so.

He'd been so close to the end of the first draft, he'd pushed to finish so he could send it to Noah. His friend was usually good at determining which projects were worth pursuing. He must have fallen asleep.

"Gracie?" He checked the living room first since she loved sneaking extra screen time.

"Mackenzie?" He peeked into Gracie's bedroom. Not finding them, he backtracked to his office and called Mackenzie's cell.

"Where are you guys?"

She sounded out of breath. "We're on our way back to the house. Gracie, slow down!"

"Not as easy as you thought to be a parent, is it?" Xavier scrubbed a hand over his face. What a stupid thing to say. "I'm sorry. I didn't mean that."

The woman had cooked dinner and picked up the slack for him while he'd holed up in his office.

"You're right. It's not."

"Emmy." How was he supposed to get himself out of this? He'd stuffed his foot so far in his mouth, he needed surgery to remove it.

"I truly didn't mean that the way it came out. I just meant Gracie's a lot of work. She wears me out most days."

She sighed. "It's okay, Xavier. We're at the door. I'd appreciate it if you'd let us in."

He rushed to the front door.

"Daddy!" Gracie threw herself at him and he caught her. "Emmy's the strongest mommy in the park."

His eyes cut to Mackenzie. She refused to meet his gaze.

"The children assumed—"

"She was the fastest person on the monkey bars." Gracie pretended to hold on to a bar and hopped a few feet. "I want to be just like her when I grow up."

"I-I—" Mackenzie lifted a hand to her mouth. "I have to go." She whirled toward the door, but not before he caught the shimmer of tears in her eyes.

He'd made her cry. The realization was a kick in the gut. He had to make it up to her. He snatched open the door and ran down the steps, spinning in both directions, hoping to glimpse her. Nothing.

"Daddy. Are you listening to me?" Gracie had followed him outside and stood with her hands on akimbo.

"I'm sorry, Gracie-mine." How much should he tell her? Since he was determined to be as honest with her as possible, he went with the truth. "I missed the last thing you said because I was worried about Miss Mackenzie."

"Emmy. She asked us to call her Emmy."

He bit back a smile. He could learn a lot from his daughter about how to treat others.

"Emmy." He squatted down to her. "There were tears in her eyes, and I wanted to make sure she was okay."

Gracie's face crumpled. "I made Emmy cry?"

"No, sweetie, I'm sure…" He wasn't sure of anything. "Sometimes grown-ups are sad for other reasons."

Gracie's face was solemn. "It's because she's alone for Christmas. Daddy, we're her Christmas family. We should cheer her up."

"Great idea. What do you suggest?"

"Cake and ice cream."

He chuckled and swung his daughter into his arms as he stood. "Are you sure that's not what you'd want?"

"Uh-huh." She nodded solemnly. "That always makes me feel better. I'm sure Emmy would like it, too."

He headed toward the house. "Excellent point. Maybe we can put some other things with it." An idea tickled the back of his mind.

* * *

It took a bit of finessing—mostly, convincing Ruby to package the meals he'd purchased in to-go containers rather than plating them to serve—but, less than two hours after Mackenzie had left his house in tears, he stood outside her door.

He took a deep breath and looked down at Gracie, who clutched the container of cupcakes they'd picked up at The Sweet Tooth.

"Ready?"

"Of course, Daddy." Gracie sighed as if she was carrying the burdens of the entire world. "Knock on the door."

He chuckled and did as she asked. Mackenzie answered the door in a pair of leggings and an oversized sweater. Mercy.

"Xavier?"

Homebody Mackenzie made him want to cuddle up somewhere with her.

"You're doing it again, Daddy."

"Sorry." Xavier shook his head and hefted the basket before Gracie exposed all his secrets. "We brought you dinner."

A slow smile crept across her face. "You did?"

"It was my idea." Gracie beamed up at Emmy. "There's ice cream and cake."

Mackenzie chuckled and bent to hug Gracie. "Let's hurry through dinner, then we can get to dessert."

She stepped back to let them in. Xavier glanced around the entry hall, attention captured by a beautiful antique clock.

"Wow. That thing still works?"

"Only took a gazillion hours to restore." She chuckled. "My family owns an antique shop in Cinnamon Hill. My father and I also do restorations."

"That must take a lot of skills."

She shrugged. "I guess. Why don't we put the ice cream in

the freezer before it melts into mush?"

"I hate mushy ice cream." Gracie slipped her hand into Emmy's.

"Me too."

Dinner was a lot of fun. Gracie kept them laughing with knock-knock jokes and one-liners. Mackenzie fit into their little family as if she'd been custom-made for the role.

Was this why he'd moved to Orange Valley? Not for all the other valid reasons, but for him to meet Mackenzie? Or for him to realize how much he craved companionship?

"Dad-dy!" Gracie's voice brimmed with frustration.

"I'm sorry, Gracie-mine. What did you say?" He refocused his attention on his daughter.

"Sometimes it's okay to say your inside thoughts out loud."

He grinned. "Was that what you wanted to tell me?"

"No." She huffed out a breath. "May I have my screen time now? I've been good all day." She clasped her hands under her chin. "Please?"

"It's Emmy's house." He looked at Mackenzie. "You'd need her permission."

Gracie switched her pleading gaze to Mackenzie.

Mackenzie chuckled. "Sure. I wouldn't want to be the reason Gracie doesn't get her screen time. Let me set it up for you." Mackenzie pushed away from the table.

"I don't need help." Gracie plopped her hands on her hips. "I'm a big girl. I can do it myself."

"I'm sure you can." Mackenzie smoothed a hand over Gracie's braids. He'd finally made an appointment to have her hair styled and her cornrows were freshly done. "Let me come with you, just in case. Okay?"

"Fine," Gracie spoke the word on a puff of air.

Gracie followed Mackenzie out of the room and Xavier began stacking the dishes they'd used for dinner beside the sink.

"Oh, you don't have to do that." Mackenzie rushed over to put a hand on his arm.

"It's okay." He grinned down at her. "Since I spent most of my life not cooking, I'm an excellent busboy."

She had the most beautiful eyes—eyes he could stare into all night.

"Mackenzie—"

"Emmy."

"Emmy."

What did he want to say? That he wanted to kiss her, to find out if her lips tasted as sweet as the treats they'd had for dessert. "I really wish we had some mistletoe."

Her eyes dropped to his mouth, and Xavier's heart galloped out of control.

"Oh?" Her tongue darted out to moisten her lips. "You'd kiss someone who hated you?"

He angled his body toward her. "I've sensed a change in the last couple of days." He slid his hands down her arms until he clasped her hands. "Was I wrong?"

"No." She shifted until she was so close, he drew in her sweet vanilla scent with every breath. "I don't hate you."

"Good. I don't hate you, either." He dipped his head to press his lips to the area below her ear. She shivered and leaned into him.

"Xavier."

He pressed a kiss to the other side. Mackenzie's hands clutched his shoulders. "Gracie."

His daughter's name was a bucket of ice water in the face.

What was he doing? Seducing a woman in the kitchen? Okay, stealing a kiss was not a seduction, but his daughter could come in any second. He disentangled himself from her with reluctance.

"You're right." He took a few steps back. "You should come to dinner tomorrow."

"I can't." She shook her head. "You should spend Christmas with family." Sorrow was etched on her features.

"Emmy." He gave into the urge and caressed her cheek.

"If you knew what I'd done—"

"Shh." He pressed a finger on her lips. "We'll talk about that another day, after Christmas. Gracie and I have adopted you as our Christmas family and want to spend the day with you."

Tears welled in Mackenzie's eyes.

"Please don't cry." Her tears threatened to mangle his insides. "Say you'll spend Christmas with us."

"On one condition." Her lips trembled into a smile. "Promise you'll have at least one sprig of mistletoe."

"Deal." There'd be so much mistletoe at his house that she'd believe he had a grove.

Nineteen

Chapter 19

Madison stuffed the last wrapped gift into her oversized tote. This would be the first Christmas when Mackenzie and Madison would be in the same country and not spend it together.

Still, a smile stole over her face as she anticipated spending time with Xavier and Gracie. She scanned Mackenzie's guest room. Had she missed anything?

The passion between her and Xavier made her eager to discover what it would be like to kiss him.

"Madison?"

She yelped, whirling toward the voice. Her sister chuckled.

"Mackenzie?" Madison shook her head. "What are you doing here?"

Her sister was supposed to be safely in Cinnamon Hill—away from the house of cards she was building in Orange Valley.

Concern was etched on her sister's features. "I was worried

about you."

Guilt flooded through her. "I'm fine."

She grabbed the tote and brushed past her sister. How would she convince Mackenzie to stay behind while she went for dinner at Xavier's? Because she was having dinner with Xavier and Gracie.

Madison stumbled to a halt when she spotted the intimidating man in the entry room. Her eyes widened. "What is he doing here?"

She whipped her head to stare at Mackenzie. Had she told her sister he'd shown up at the house? She couldn't remember. It had been so long since she'd thought of that incident with Cameron Grant.

"Did he follow you?" This wasn't one of those cases where a man didn't accept when a woman said no, was it? She grabbed Mackenzie's hand.

"It's okay," Mackenzie spoke in a soothing voice. "Cameron and I are together." A soft smile crept over Mackenzie's face as she stared at the real estate mogul, who was smiling at her sister with the same lovesick expression.

"What do you mean 'together'?" It took a second for Madison's brain to pick up on Mackenzie's meaning. Her eyebrows shot up. "You mean *together* together?"

Mackenzie nodded, her mouth curving into a smile.

"He's the mystery guy?" Madison was almost shrieking at her sister. He'd been telling the truth about kissing Mackenzie? Why hadn't her sister told her she was dating the billionaire?

"Mackenzie," Cameron Grant gestured to the door behind him. "I'm going to—"

"No," Mackenzie bolted across the room and grabbed his hand. "You can't leave. You're spending Christmas Day with me and Madison."

"Not me." Madison shook her head. "I have plans."

"What do you mean?"

Madison shifted from one foot to the next. This was why she hadn't wanted Mackenzie here. How was she supposed to explain this without hurting her sister?

"I'm having dinner with a friend."

Mackenzie gaped at her. "You made plans without me?"

Madison's gaze darted away from Mackenzie's. "I didn't think you'd come back to Orange Valley for Christmas."

Mackenzie's voice was soft. "We always spend Christmas together."

"I know, but—"

"I checked out of a penthouse suite and took a flight to be here with you."

Madison's eyebrows winged up. Just what was Cameron Grant up to with her sister? She and Mackenzie needed to have a heart-to-heart. Just not today.

God, why was this so hard? Can I just have one Christmas with Gracie and Xavier?

Okay, she wanted more, but she was willing to settle for one. A single happy moment she'd cherish forever before she confessed everything.

"You can't come."

Madison blocked out her sister's hurt. She needed this day with her Christmas family. She put the bag beside the front door and hurried to the kitchen, Mackenzie on her heels.

"Who did you say was hosting the party?"

She wasn't in the mood for the third degree as she grabbed anything Xavier could use for the Christmas dinner. She hadn't even asked if he wanted her to help him cook. After all, the man had just mastered brown stewed chicken and steamed rice.

"You don't know him."

Mackenzie's eyebrows shot up. Oh, dear. Madison had revealed too much information. How did she get out of this pickle?

Mackenzie laid a hand on her arm. "Emmy, what's going on?"

Madison laughed, hoping her sister wouldn't pick up on the false notes.

"Nothing." Madison's eyes shifted away from Mackenzie's. She hated keeping secrets from her twin.

Really? Madison's inner voice piped up. *Cause you've been doing a pretty good job of it so far.*

She played it off. "You can't tell me you're not happy to spend time with the handsome billionaire. Isn't he your client?"

Mackenzie pressed her palms to her cheeks. "Yes. No."

When Mackenzie confessed she was in love with Cameron, Madison was almost as shocked as the man himself.

"I'll leave you guys to talk." She crammed a few more items into the bulging shopping bag before hustling past Cameron Grant and out of the house. She trusted her sister to work herself out of that situation. Meanwhile, she had a mistletoe kiss to secure.

* * *

The door flew open before she could knock. Xavier grabbed the bags from her and stashed them on the floor. Madison entered the house and drew in a deep breath.

"Hmm, something smells good." She reached for the lapels

of her coat.

"Allow me." He stepped behind her and slipped his hands in the place of hers. "Something smells delicious." He dropped a kiss at the sensitive spot behind her ear and she leaned into him.

"Xavier…"

Why did this man make her yearn for things she couldn't have?

He twirled her in his arms until she was facing him.

"Mistletoe." He pointed to the bunch of artificial red berries above their heads.

A smile stole over her face. "Does it still count if the berries aren't real?" She twisted her arms around his neck.

"That depends." He tugged her closer.

"On what?" Man, it was getting hard to breathe.

"How real you think my kisses are."

"Gracie—"

"Is enjoying an early screen time which means I have about two minutes to steal a kiss from a beautiful woman before she comes searching for me."

"Can this kiss be from any beautiful woman?"

"No." Xavier's eyes met hers. "Only you."

Oh, my. If she hadn't already become a puddle of need from being in his arms, the expression in his eyes would have melted her.

"Emmy." He tipped her face up to his and met her lips with his.

It was a good thing she'd been holding on to him as waves of sensation crashed over her. She moaned and clutched his shoulders tighter.

"What are you guys doing?"

She stifled a groan. No, it was too soon. She wanted the full two minutes he'd promised her. She tugged away from him but Xavier's arm tightened around her waist.

"Mistletoe." Xavier pointed over their heads.

"Oh. That's okay then." Gracie pouted. "I was hoping it was because you were falling madly in love with each other."

"Why don't you take Emmy's bag of gifts and put them with the others around the Christmas tree?" Xavier kept his arms firmly around her waist.

"Ooh, presents." Gracie peered into the bag. "Are they all mine?"

"Alana Grace."

"I'm going, Daddy." Gracie grabbed the straps of the bag and dragged it across the floor.

The second Gracie disappeared, Madison dropped her head against his shoulder. "How do single parents date when they have a child that age?"

"I'm not sure. This is my first attempt." Xavier tipped her head toward his. "I think we're doing okay, don't you?"

Madison's eyes widened. Xavier thought they were dating? Images of them spending time together flashed through her mind. They were dating.

"Emmy?"

And he didn't know her real name.

"Too fast?" He arched a brow, his eyes filled with concern.

"No." She'd worry about everything tomorrow. "Too little kissing." She twined her arms behind his head.

He grinned and lowered his head to hers. "Your wish is my command."

* * *

Madison's brow knitted when Xavier uncovered the serving trays in the center of the table. Roasted turkey, escoveitched fish, and steamed rice and peas. There was also a tossed salad and creamy mashed potatoes.

"You did all of this?"

The man had been holding out on her.

"Eh, no." Xavier massaged the back of his neck. "Apparently, there's a company that prepares Christmas dinner for the domestically-challenged. They even come and set everything up for you."

"Wow." Madison's eyes darted back to the meal. This must have been expensive.

"It's our Christmas present." Gracie bounced in her chair.

"Excuse me?"

"Yeah," Xavier winced. "My parents and in-laws came together on this gift. They didn't trust me to ensure Gracie had an enjoyable Christmas meal."

"Hey," she rested a hand on his arm. "Gracie would have been happy with a bowl of cereal if she got to spend the day with you."

She truly believed that. The man may be hopeless in the kitchen, but he loves Gracie.

"That's true, Daddy, but maybe I'd have asked for ice cream too. Can we eat now?"

"Soon." Xavier stood at the head of the table and gestured for her and Gracie to take a seat on either side. "Gracie, do you remember why we celebrate Christmas?"

He held out a hand for each of them, they slid their hands in his.

"Uh-huh." The girl nodded. "To tell Jesus thanks for saving us."

"That's right, Gracie-mine." Xavier smiled at Gracie. "God loved us so much, He sent His Son Jesus to live with us." He turned to her. "What happened next, Emmy?"

Madison cleared her throat, overwhelmed because Xavier included her in his family's routine. "When Jesus grew up, He died for our sins."

"Exactly." Xavier continued. "Christmas isn't about the presents we get for each other. It's about the greatest gift of all—Jesus Christ."

Joy flooded Madison's heart. God's gift to her was one she could never repay. Her only response should be worship, not surliness when she didn't get her way.

I'm sorry, God. Thank You for the gift of Your Son and for not treating me as my sins deserve.

Twenty

Chapter 20

Xavier blinked at the couple on his front step.

"Mom? Dad? What are you guys doing here?"

"Surprise!" Diane Washington threw her arms open, and he leaned down to hug her.

"Didn't we agree to separate Christmases this year?"

His mom rolled her eyes. "That's why we weren't here *yesterday*." She pushed past him into the house. "Meanwhile, you've forgotten every lick of manners I taught you."

His mother looked around the house. "Jacqui did a good job with this place." Diane skewered him with a glance. "Are you planning to marry that girl?"

Xavier squeezed the back of his neck. "I don't think of her that way."

"That's what I told you, Diane." Carl Washington nodded. "I figured it out the minute she came back to Idlewood acting like someone had kicked her favorite puppy."

Xavier winced. "I didn't know she'd felt that way until the last time she was here." He'd only suspected it until his father's words.

"I know that boy," his father clapped him on the shoulder. "We didn't raise you to dally with a woman's heart."

His father's words made him feel worse. He should have realized Jacqui thought of him as more than her brother-in-law.

His mother arched a brow. "When are you going to marry again? Alicia's been dead for three years and Gracie needs a mother."

Sheesh. She'd been here five minutes and already Xavier was contemplating ducking into his office and pretending to work.

"Mom."

She waved a hand. "You were grieving, but life goes on. You can fall in love with someone else without dishonoring Alicia's memory."

Xavier swallowed. How had his mom identified the root of his struggles? He'd only figured it out himself.

"Now, enough jawing with you." Diane plopped her hands on her hips. "Where's my grandbaby?"

"Mom, it's 7 a.m., Gracie's asleep."

His mom was usually up long before dawn, her sewing machine clattering along as she completed orders for her customers or family members.

His father gave him an amused look. "I held her back as long as I could or she would have been here a minute after midnight."

Xavier chuckled. "It's good to see you, Mom."

"Of course it is." She patted his back, already thinking of the next thing she could do. "I'll make breakfast."

He wasn't one to pass up a free meal but—"You know I can do that, right? Gracie and I haven't starved since we moved to Orange Valley."

"Oh, pooh." Diane waved her hand. "We can do better than cereal."

Within an hour, Diane had fried a batch of festivals and cooked up a pot of ackee and saltfish.

"I'll get Gracie." He woke his daughter and got her ready in record time. He headed toward the dining room. "I have a surprise for you."

She smiled up at him. "Is Emmy here for breakfast again?"

"Who's Emmy?"

His parents exchanged glances, their eyes full of curiosity.

"Gammy? Pops?" Gracie flew across the room and threw herself at her grandparents. That should buy him some time. From his mother's expression, his reprieve would be short.

* * *

As soon as breakfast was done, he'd bolted out of the house to avoid answering questions he didn't want to. Xavier took his time, enjoying a few hours when he didn't have to worry about Gracie.

Maybe he could convince Mackenzie to spend the afternoon with him. It'd give them time to be together without their mini-chaperone, and confirm that they both wanted the same thing. Then he'd have something definite to tell his mom about the woman he was kinda dating.

As if conjured by his thoughts, he spotted Emmy in front of Ruby's Place. If that wasn't providence, he didn't know what was. He lengthened his stride.

"Emmy."

Mackenzie pulled out her phone and took a picture of the door, without responding to him. He pressed closer, almost bumping into her as she whirled away from the door.

"Mackenzie?"

"Yes?" She paused mid-stride and scanned him from head to toe, a polite smile on her face. Why was she acting like they were strangers?

"What are you doing here?" He smiled, hoping to trigger an answering one.

"Uhm," she pointed over her shoulder. "Scavenger hunt."

"Do you want to hang out for a few hours? No chaperone." They'd had a wonderful day yesterday, and he had a hunger for a few of those kisses with no Gracie to interrupt.

She backed away. "Uh, no." She waggled her fingers. "Nice seeing you again."

Xavier stared after her. What just happened? Had he scared her away? Mackenzie ran into the arms of a man built like a linebacker. And it was as though someone had punched him in the gut.

Had he misunderstood Mackenzie's attention? Was it possible she'd only been interested in Gracie? Or had she been biding her time until someone better came along? Bile rose in his throat. He was no longer eager for a few hours alone.

Xavier skulked into his house, hoping to avoid running into anyone. The memory of doing the same to avoid Jacqui caused an ironic smile to twist his mouth. Maybe he should marry his sister-in-law. At least she cared about him. Then Gracie would have a mother who loved her and he'd have a wife who wouldn't sneak around behind his back.

He made it to his office without bumping into anyone and

closed the door behind him. A faint vanilla scent lingered in the air—even what should have been his haven was tainted by memories of her.

"Get over it, Xavier."

Unless he planned to move again, he'd have to get used to memories of Mackenzie bombarding him until he got over her.

He turned on the game console and loaded an open-world game he'd played several times. Beating down a couple of bosses was just what he needed to forget about her for a few minutes.

He wasn't sure how long he'd been playing when someone knocked on the door. Before he could answer, the door popped open and his mom came inside. He should have locked the door. Maybe if he ignored her, she'd assume he was working and go away.

Diane tapped her foot. "You've played this game before, Xavier."

He muffled a sigh and paused the game. "What is it, Mom?" He kept his voice respectful. Being heartbroken wasn't an excuse to be rude.

A sly smile crept over her face. "I can see why you and Gracie are taken with her. Your Emmy's beautiful."

She was here? He stood, his traitorous heart beating a mile a minute at the thought of seeing her again. He brushed past his mother without a word.

Mackenzie had changed out of her earlier outfit of jeans and sweater into one of those sweater dresses he loved. Today's was moss green, worn over green tights.

She and Gracie sat on one end of the dining table, squaring off against his father in a game of domino. She was explaining the concept of matching numbers to Gracie.

For a second, he wanted to go back in time. To walk more slowly so he wouldn't see her stop at Ruby's. To turn away before she'd stepped into another man's arms. But he had seen her and he couldn't forget.

"What are you doing here?"

His voice was so harsh that even Gracie's mouth popped open.

"Daddy, why are you growling at Emmy?"

"Yes, Xavier." Mackenzie smiled up at him. "I thought you and I were friends."

"You are not my friend."

Tears filled Mackenzie's eyes, and he clenched his fists. He would not reach for her.

She pushed back her chair. "I should go."

"No." Diane rushed into the room. "You should stay and give my son a piece of your mind." She hustled Gracie out of her chair. "Acting like he doesn't know better." She glared at Carl until he stood as well. "You don't leave until he apologizes." Diane patted Mackenzie's cheek. "Come on, Gracie."

Gracie threw her arms around Mackenzie's legs. "I love you, Emmy." She glared at Xavier. "Daddy's being mean."

Gee. She was the one who'd done something wrong. Why was he the one being punished?

Because he hadn't told them what happened.

He opened his mouth to tell them what he'd seen, then snapped it shut.

He who answers a matter before he hears it, It is folly and shame to him.

Maybe he should listen to what she had to say before shutting her out of his and Gracie's life. Fool that he was, he wanted her to have a plausible explanation.

Mackenzie wrapped her arms around herself as his family traipsed out of the room. He stared after them. How would he fill the Mackenzie-sized hole in his daughter's life?

"Xavier?"

He steeled himself to meet her gaze.

"What's going on?"

"I saw you today." At her blank stare, he continued. "In front of Ruby's?"

"Uhm," her brow furrowed. "I don't remember going near Ruby's, but it's been a long day." She shook her head. "Why didn't you say hello?"

Xavier cocked his head. Was she truly pretending not to know what he was talking about?

"I did." He spoke through gritted teeth.

"I didn't see you today, Xavier. Not until I came to your house."

He scoffed. "Let me guess, the woman I saw earlier was your twin sister. Is that what you're trying to convince me?"

She tittered. "Uhm, funny thing about that." Her eyes darted around the room.

Xavier folded his arms across his chest, curious about what she'd say. Mackenzie straightened her shoulders.

"Uhm, yes. I think maybe you did see my twin sister today."

Twenty-One

Chapter 21

Xavier snorted. "You and I had the potential to become something," he held out his hand, and opened it wide, "more." He dropped his hand.

Madison had imagined several scenarios about what would happen when she finally confessed, but this had never been one of them.

"I'm telling the truth."

"It would have been easier if you'd told me there was someone else you were interested in. This," he gestured to her, "story you've made up, insults both of us."

Xavier shook his head and walked away. Madison gaped at the door he'd disappeared through. Did she follow him? Beg him to listen to her? How would she prove to him she wasn't lying?

She winced. She had lied and was still lying to him about so many things.

Diane came into the room. "I take it things didn't go as you'd hoped."

How much should she admit to this woman whose loyalty would be toward her son?

"Not quite." Madison lifted her shoulders. "He didn't believe me."

Diane met her gaze. "Let me guess. He didn't give you a chance to explain."

She shook her head.

Diane touched Madison's arm. "He'll need time to process. If you and my son plan to be together, you must understand this about him."

"Oh, no! Xavier and I are not..." Her eyes widened. What was she supposed to say? Especially with that expression of amused pity on Diane's face?

"Please, dear, don't patronize me. I saw the way you looked at him and the way he was gobbling you up with his eyes. The two of you may not admit what you feel about each other, but it will come out soon enough. Love doesn't stay suppressed for long."

Madison almost staggered under the weight of Diane's observation. Love? Surely she wasn't in love with Xavier. She couldn't be. Not with the amount of deception between them.

He didn't lie.

Oh, dear. Her eyes flicked to the door again. She'd ruined any chance they had of being together by not being honest with him. The thought of never seeing Xavier—or Gracie—again broke her heart.

"I have to go." She rushed past Diane and out of Xavier's house before the first tear fell.

* * *

"You've been in a funk since you came home yesterday," Mackenzie commented. "Are you alright?"

"I'm fine." She dropped the handful of peas she'd shelled into the bowl between them.

Mackenzie was cooking dinner for Cameron and had gotten up early to bake. Madison couldn't wait to have a bite of her sister's signature Christmas cake, although she planned to have dinner in her room. No need to be a downer two nights in a row. The cake's fragrance made the mindless task more bearable.

"Madison," Mackenzie laid a hand on hers to still her movement. "You know you can tell me anything, right?"

"Yes." Except for the secret she'd kept all these years. How was she supposed to come clean about those things? She stared into the face so like hers and forced a smile.

She'd tell Mackenzie everything, but not now. Not when Mackenzie was basking in the throes of new love. And certainly not when her sister's new boyfriend was on his way to the house. Again.

Cameron spent so much time at the house that Madison had become a third wheel.

"Have I told you how happy I am for you and Cameron?"

Mackenzie wrinkled her nose. "No. I wondered if you were upset about it."

Madison's eyes widened. "Upset? Why would you think that?"

"I don't know." Mackenzie shrugged. "You were kind of grumpy last night. I wasn't sure if it was because you came home in a crummy mood or for some other reason."

Madison dropped her gaze. She needed to up her game if she was going to convince her sister she was okay with her being with Cameron.

"I'm happy for you." She truly was. It was just hard to be all enthusiastic with a broken heart.

"Okay." Mackenzie's voice was soft. "I still sense that you're keeping secrets."

Madison tilted a brow.

"Alright, so I kept one from you, too. I didn't tell you about Cameron because, for a while, I wasn't sure what was happening. I thought he liked you."

"Me?" Madison's hand flew to her chest. "I've never—"

"I know that." Mackenzie mock-glared at her. "But that's the problem with switching places." She gestured between them. "You're never sure if the person is talking about you or your twin."

She winced at the truth of Mackenzie's statement. She'd made a mockery of her relationship with Xavier because she'd hidden behind Mackenzie's identity.

A soft smile stole over her sister's face. "This thing with Cameron happened so fast." Mackenzie made a face. "I didn't mean to keep it from you. I'm sorry."

"It's okay. I know there are no secrets between us." Madison almost choked on the words.

Lying lips are an abomination unto the Lord.

She groaned. The weight of carrying this secret was pressing her into the ground.

"Mackenzie—"

"Madison—"

They spoke at the same time and then grinned at each other.

"You go first." Madison waved at her sister. It would give her time to find the perfect words.

"There is a secret I'm still keeping from you."

Her eyebrows shot up. "What?"

"I—"

There was a loud banging on the front door. Madison groaned. "Hold that thought."

The oven timer dinged. "You get that," Madison told her sister. "I'll get the door. I don't enjoy eating burnt fruit cake."

Mackenzie chuckled and tugged on her oven mitts. Madison hurried to the front door to let Cameron in.

"Hi."

Not Cameron. Xavier and Gracie stood on the front step.

"Uhm," she hadn't expected to see him so soon. Maybe not never. "What are you doing here?"

"We came to visit you, Emmy." Gracie blinked up at her. "Aren't you happy to see us?"

"Of course, I'm always happy to see you, pumpkin pie." Her lips tipped upward.

"You left your coat at the house." Xavier held up her autumn-colored coat. She hadn't missed it. She'd been in such a hurry to leave last night, she'd forgotten it.

"I—" she cleared her throat. "Thank you." She reached for the coat, taking care not to touch him.

"Can we come inside? I'd like to hear what you wanted to tell me earlier."

Now? This was the worst possible time. A vehicle pulled up at the gate and Cameron got out. Scratch that. *This* was the worst possible moment.

"I—" her eyes flicked up to the man walking toward them.

Xavier glanced over his shoulder, then back at her. "Never mind." His mouth tightened. "I can't compete with Cameron

Grant. Let's go home, Gracie."

Xavier spun, almost bumping into Cameron.

"Madison, who was at the door?"

"Hi, Princess." Cameron brushed past her, his eyes fixed on Mackenzie.

"Daddy," Gracie's whisper was reverent. "There are two of them." Gracie pointed at Mackenzie.

Xavier's eyes widened. "You were telling the truth."

Madison nodded. The tiny movement was all she could manage as her two worlds collided.

"Madison?" Mackenzie's gaze dropped to Gracie. "Whose child is that?"

Xavier frowned at Madison. "Who's Madison?"

Cameron frowned at her. "You didn't tell him?"

Xavier's voice got louder in his confusion. "Tell me what?"

Mackenzie's laugh held a tinge of bitterness. "It turns out my sister's good at keeping secrets."

"Mackenzie—" she reached a hand toward her twin.

"No." Mackenzie took a step back.

"Will someone please tell me what's going on? Mackenzie?" Xavier's eyes searched her face.

Madison opened her mouth to answer, but no words came. She swallowed and tried again. Her eyes filled and tears spilled down her cheeks. "My name's not Mackenzie."

Twenty-Two

Chapter 22

The four words rocked Xavier's world. "What?"

"My name's Madison Porter. Mackenzie's my twin."

His eyes switched to the woman, who was a replica of the one in front of him.

"Emmy?" Gracie's voice wobbled. "What's going on ?"

"I'm sorry, sweetie. I-I lied to you and your father."

The words shook Xavier out of his stupor. "Why?"

"Sorry." The billionaire tycoon approached him. "We should take this inside." Cameron Grant glanced over his shoulder at Mackenzie? "Something tells me this conversation requires sitting down."

Xavier perched on an armchair, too numb to process much of what was going on. He tugged his daughter against him. He was sure of two things. One, that he wouldn't like much of what would come next, and two, it would have a tremendous impact on him and Gracie.

Cameron Grant sat with his arm around one of the women on the long couch, leaving Emmy—was that even her name?—to sit in the other armchair. She clutched her hands in front of her and refused to make eye contact with anyone.

"Emmy?" Gracie's voice wobbled.

"That's not her name," Xavier growled the words. How had he spent all that time with her and not realize she was lying to him?

Madison-Mackenzie smiled at Gracie. At least, she tried to. Only one corner of her mouth curved upward.

"My family calls me Emmy. It's a nickname for Madison."

"Oh," Gracie said the word with a pop.

Well, at least that was something.

"I'm still waiting to hear why you lied to me." Xavier steeled himself against the pain that flashed across her face at his harsh tone. She did not deserve his sympathy.

"Mackenzie and I switched places for a couple of weeks."

"Like in It Takes Two?" Gracie wriggled out of the circle of his arms.

"Yes, Gracie." Emmy cut her eyes toward her sister. "It was kind of like that."

"Why?" Mackenzie sounded as angry as he did. "I know it has something to do with her."

Xavier frowned. Who was Mackenzie talking about? His eyes flitted to her. She was staring at Gracie. His heart pounded. *Everyone* was staring at Gracie. What did she have to do with anything?

"Gracie, it's time to go." He stood and held out his hand, expecting his daughter to comply.

"Sir? I'm sorry, but you can't leave." Mackenzie shook her

head. "Madison needs to answer the question, and I think you need to hear what she has to say."

No, he was pretty sure he didn't want to know. But what good would it be to bury his head in the sand? Isn't that what he'd been doing these past three years? Hiding? It hadn't served him well. He'd isolated himself from his family and insulated himself from other people's emotions. He sighed.

"My name is Xavier Washington."

"I'm Mackenzie Porter," she pointed to herself. "Cameron Grant." She gestured to the man, who still had his arm around her.

"Now that we're all acquainted—"

"You forgot about me."

Had he ever been glad for his daughter's outspokenness?

"I'm Alana Grace, but you can call me Gracie." She held out both sides of her dress and dipped. Mackenzie's lips quirked.

"Nice to meet you, Gracie."

"Say, Gracie," Cameron squatted in front of her. "What do you say we get some ice cream?" He looked up at Xavier. "If that's alright with your dad."

"I love ice cream." Gracie turned pleading eyes to his. "Can I get ice cream, Daddy?"

What he wanted was to take his daughter out of this house and forget he'd ever met Emmy or whatever her name was. But Mackenzie was right. He needed to hear the entire story.

He cleared his throat. "Sure."

Cameron stood and took Gracie's hand. "We'll be in the kitchen." Cameron pointed in the direction while holding Xavier's gaze. "Come for her when you're ready."

Xavier tipped his chin in grudging respect. His eyes followed them out of the room, before turning to Emmy, who clutched the armrests as if her life depended on it.

"Okay, Madison, let's hear it."

Mackenzie's voice was stern. Was she the older twin? Things he should have known about the woman he was halfway in love with.

Madison licked her lips. "I'm not sure where to start."

"Why don't you start with why you insisted we switch places or why Alana Grace looks exactly like we did at that age?"

What? Xavier dropped into the armchair he'd vacated. "What is she talking about?"

Madison's eyes filled with tears. "I have to go further back than that." She briefly met his gaze. "Our parents own an antique shop."

She'd told him that. At least something she'd said hadn't been a lie. .

"I got a scholarship to a school in Italy where I studied antique restoration. I met a guy."

"Madison," Mackenzie said her sister's name on a breath.

Xavier had a sinking feeling in his gut.

"Sergio. He was a few years older, and his attention was flattering." Madison's expression softened at the memory.

"He took me to see the sights—not the usual tourist attractions, the places only locals visited. Within a few weeks, I thought I was in love. He, we—" Madison dropped her gaze to the linked fingers in her lap. "I gave myself to him."

"Madison, no!" Mackenzie's voice trembled with emotion.

Xavier was numb, waiting for the rest of what Madison had to say. He'd already guessed the truth.

"He made me feel special." Madison turned her tear-stained face to Mackenzie. "I thought we were going to be married."

The brute. Men like Sergio preyed on the innocent.

"When I told him I was pregnant, he claimed he couldn't possibly be my baby's father, though I'd never been with anyone else." Madison's hands clenched into fists. "Then he disappeared."

"Of course you hadn't." Mackenzie's defense of her sister was fierce as she flew across the room to kneel at Madison's feet. "He's a horrible man. Why didn't you tell us, Em?"

Madison snorted. "And prove to Dad he'd been right? You know how much he hated sending me to Italy."

"You should have told *me*, Emmy." Mackenzie insisted. "We don't keep secrets from each other."

"I know." Tears spilled down Madison's cheek. "I'm sorry."

"What does this have to do with my daughter?"

Emmy recoiled at the harshness of his tone. It couldn't be helped. He needed her to say what he'd already surmised.

"Gracie's my daughter." Madison stared at a spot beyond his shoulder. "I wanted her to grow up on Saturn Island and found an agency that accepted my terms."

It explained a lot, including her emotional response to the Memory Line.

"What does that mean? You plan to take my daughter away from me?"

"No!" Madison met his eyes. "You're Gracie's father, and she loves you. It's just that..." Her lips trembled. "I recently found out I probably can't have any more children, I wondered—I wanted to meet her. To make sure she was okay."

"You couldn't have just contacted me the way a normal person would have?"

She flinched. "I did. You didn't respond to any of my letters."

"I never," Xavier began. He wouldn't have rejected an overture from Gracie's birth mother. It was an open adoption, so the option was there. He and Alicia had pondered whether to involve Gracie's birth mom in her life or not.

But there had been those eighteen months after her death when he'd refused to read any correspondence. He'd either sent them back unopened or thrown them in the trash.

After that, he'd only opened correspondence from people and companies he'd known. Foolish, but he'd had enough of people's sympathy and then their insistence that he should move on with his life.

Had he tossed Madison's letter without recognizing its significance? How many other important missives had he missed?

"Maybe." He stroked his chin. "But you showing up here, pretending to care about Gracie," and about him, "is unacceptable."

"I'm sorry. Okay? What do you want me to say? I never intended to deceive you. My plan was to watch you from a distance and maybe get a glimpse of Gracie."

"What changed?" Mackenzie laid a hand on her sister's arm.

"Brianna asked me to help with VBS."

Mackenzie's eyes widened.

"She thought I was you. Then I went that first day and fell in love with Gracie all over again." Madison met Xavier's eyes, her expression fierce. "I may have given her to you to raise, but I've always loved her. I never stopped loving her and I never will."

Twenty-Three

Chapter 23

"That might be so, Madison, or whatever your name is, but Gracie's *my* daughter. I have the papers *you* signed that made it legal." Xavier stalked out of the room, returning a few moments with Gracie and Cameron trailing behind.

"Emmy." The little girl pulled away from her father and threw herself into Madison's arms. "Daddy says you're going away and I'll never see you again. Is that true?"

Madison's eyes flew to Xavier's. That was his solution? He didn't intend to tell Gracie she was her birth mother?

She's a child, Madison, and this is the path you chose.

She held back her tears. "Yes, Gracie. I'll be returning home."

"But this isn't what was supposed to happen. You and Daddy were to fall in love and get married. Then you'd be my new mommy, and I'd be your daughter forever."

Kill her now. Gracie's words pulverized her heart. Why hadn't she been honest? If she had, maybe things would have played out how they had in Gracie's fantasies.

"I don't want you to go, Emmy." Gracie sobbed. "I love you."

Gracie's tears and the child's declaration unlocked the barrier she'd built up around her own emotions.

"Hey." Madison knelt and put her arms around Gracie. "I'm sorry I have to go. I wish—" Madison swallowed the tears that clogged her throat. "I wish I didn't have to leave."

"Don't you love me, Emmy? I want you to be my new mommy because my heart always feels happy when you're near."

Oh. Madison's tears fell as freely as Gracie's now. "My heart's always happier when you're nearby, too." She knuckled away her tears.

"Enough, Gracie." Xavier's voice was gruff. "We have to go."

"Just a minute." Madison held up a shaking finger, not taking her eyes off her precious daughter. She wiped away Gracie's tears. "I love you, Alana Grace. I'll always love you."

She said the words fiercely because they were all she had to give. Madison kissed Gracie on both cheeks.

Gracie flung her arms around her neck. Why couldn't life work out like they did in a rom-com? Where every woman was the heroine of her own story with a guaranteed happy ending in three hundred pages or fewer?

Her eyes shifted to Xavier. He stood with his hands clenched, eyes dark. She unwound Gracie's arms from around her neck.

"Go with Daddy, love."

Gracie trudged toward Xavier who picked her up and stomped away without a single word.

Cameron's eyes darted between the door and Madison's. "I missed a lot."

"Not that much." Mackenzie's laugh was bitter. "My sister had an affair. Gracie is her secret baby, whom she gave up for adoption. She lied to our entire family for over five years."

Cameron's gaze flicked to Madison, full of sympathy. "Maybe she thought that was the only way."

"Our family isn't like yours, Cameron. We'd have figured it out if Madison had told us what was going on."

Cameron stiffened.

"I'm sorry." Mackenzie rested a palm on his chest. "I didn't mean that the way it sounded."

Great, now she was messing up her sister's relationship. Madison pushed to her feet. "I'm going to bed."

"Oh, no." Mackenzie wheeled around. "You and I still have things to discuss. Just," she made the waiting signal. "Stay there."

Mackenzie turned back to Cameron. "Do you mind if we do this tomorrow?"

"Sure." Cameron took Mackenzie's hands in his. "You guys can get through this. I'll be praying for you." He pulled Mackenzie into his arms and pressed a kiss to her forehead.

Madison closed her eyes. She could have had that with Xavier. Was she doomed to be a voyeur in other people's relationships?

Madison turned her back to give the couple some privacy, steeling herself for the confrontation to come. Her sister's anger and hurt would be hard to deal with, especially since she was also nursing a broken heart.

As soon as Cameron left the room, Mackenzie turned to her. "Why?"

Why what? Why'd she had an affair with Sergio? Or why had she given her daughter up for adoption? Maybe Mackenzie wanted to know why she'd hid this from her when they never had secrets between them. They kept things from their family, but not from each other. She had no answers.

"I thought I was making the right decision."

Mackenzie threw up her hands. "The right decision? In what universe did anything that happened here seem like the right decision?"

Madison rounded her shoulders. Mackenzie was right. She'd made a muck of everything. Madison clutched her stomach. Having Mackenzie mad at her was the worst feeling in the world.

"Will you ever be able to forgive me?"

Mackenzie's jaw clenched. "I don't know." She sighed. "I guess I will eventually, but it'll take time."

Madison nodded, swallowing back her tears. She'd cried enough in front of an audience tonight. She'd save the rest of her tears until she'd locked herself in Mackenzie's guestroom.

But the tears wouldn't come. All she could see was Xavier's shattered expression when she'd told him her name and Gracie's tear-stained face as her father carried her away. She'd ruined everything, including her relationship with her twin.

With her sister mad at her, she had no reason to remain in Orange Valley, the place where her heart had shattered into a million pieces. She packed her stuff and headed downstairs.

* * *

She'd thought she'd be better off in Cinnamon Hill, but she'd forgotten how silent it would be with everyone gone. She didn't even have the distraction of work since they were closed for the holidays.

She'd use the day or two before her parents returned to clear her head. Madison grabbed the keys to the store. Maybe this was the perfect time to do an inventory—something she'd always put off. She'd much rather restore an antique piece to its former glory than dust and rearrange the furniture.

It was barely seven o'clock when Madison opened the front door. She'd learned that entering through the backdoor was synonymous with competing at an Olympic field event. She did not have the mental capacity to navigate through that clutter today.

She should do something about it now that Dad wasn't here to give her grief about it. Madison flicked on the floodlights and gaped. Had someone robbed them? No.

She scanned the room, assigning price tags to every item. Everything was still here, but someone had made the shop floor into a showplace instead of the dumper fire it had been.

She dialed her sister's number. "What did you do?"

"Madison?" Mackenzie's voice was groggy. "Why are you always waking me up?"

"Maybe because you're always sleeping when I call."

"I couldn't sleep last night. What's up?"

That was her fault as well. Madison pushed away the bitter thought.

"I'm on the shop floor."

"Oh. Do you like it?"

She wasn't the one Mackenzie had to worry about. Dad would have a fit when he came home and saw what Mackenzie had done.

"Emmy?"

"Now who's keeping secrets?"

Mackenzie hissed out a breath, and Madison wanted to bite

her tongue. "Kenzie—"

"Not telling you I cleaned up the store is *nothing* like what you did. You had a secret relationship and a baby! Then you hid it for almost six years. Six years, Emmy! You put my niece up for adoption without giving me a chance to figure out how to keep her in the family."

"I know. I'm sorry."

Mackenzie exhaled—the air whooshing into the mouthpiece. "Maybe we should give ourselves some breathing space. I'll call you when I'm not so hurt, otherwise…"

They may never speak to each other again. Mackenzie hung up before Madison could think of a response.

Twenty-Four

Chapter 24

Xavier dragged himself through the front door, struggling to navigate with Gracie clinging to his neck like a koala.

"Oh, honey, you're back." His mother rushed to greet him. "Did you and Mackenzie have a pleasant talk?"

Xavier snorted. His mother *had* been playing matchmaker when she'd sent him to return Mack-Madison's cloak. When he'd left the house, he'd expected a positive ending, too.

"Gracie?" Diane's voice rose with concern as she smoothed a hand over Gracie's forehead. "What's wrong with her?"

Gracie lifted her head. "My heart hurts, Gammy."

"Xavier?" Diane's voice rose. "Shouldn't we take her to the emergency room?"

"It's nothing like that, Mom. She's just sad." A wave of tiredness washed over him. "Let me put her to bed." And figure out what to tell his mother about everything he'd learned.

Getting Gracie ready for bed was easier than normal. There was no enthusiastic retelling of stories. She didn't ask one million questions. It was as if someone had pressed the mute button.

"What story should I read for you tonight?"

"I don't want a story." Gracie climbed into bed and pulled the comforter up to her neck. "Are you sure we won't see Emmy again?"

Not as sure as he'd been twenty minutes before. The walk between Mackenzie's house and his had done much to cool his anger. So had the pain his daughter was in. How could he communicate his decision with finality when he was already doubting it?

What would happen if Gracie wanted to meet her birth mother when she turned eighteen? How would he explain to her why he'd cut her mother out of their lives?

Lord, I could use Your help. What do I say to my daughter, who's hurting? Did I make the wrong decision?

"Daddy?"

He cleared his throat. "I'm not sure, sweetie."

"Why couldn't you have fallen in love with Emmy the way I did?" Gracie folded her arms over her chest, lips pushing into a pout. "Then everyone would be happy."

He'd been more than halfway in love with Madison and had been fantasizing about making her a permanent fixture in their lives.

"Sometimes, Gracie, things don't work out the way we hope, and that will make us sad. But God is always thinking about us, searching for ways to turn a bad thing into a good one."

Even if it seemed like He'd turned away from you in the middle of your trial.

"You're right, Daddy. Jesus is my Friend. I'll ask Him to watch over Emmy. Maybe she'll change her mind and I'll get to see her again."

His daughter's maturity amazed him. Madison's deception had hurt so much that he hadn't once considered praying for her.

Had Gracie learned the art of forgiveness from his family or Alicia's? Or could it be genetic?

Didn't he owe it to his daughter to mend the bridge between her birth family and his? Could he continue to live in Orange Valley with Gracie's aunt a few houses away and not cultivate a relationship with her? Would he see Mackenzie and long for her twin sister?

Xavier pulled the door closed behind him, leaving a sliver so the light from the landing was visible through the crack.

God, did I make the right decision? What should I do next?

Why did God always become silent when you were going through the greatest tribulation? Xavier rubbed the center of his chest as he headed toward the living room, where both of his parents would be waiting. Maybe Gracie's heart pain was contagious because his chest hurt like someone had punched him in it.

* * *

"Son?" His father stepped away from the window as he approached. "Your mother says Gracie's having heart trouble, and you didn't take her to the hospital?"

His mother stood before the couch, both hands clasped together. Her eyes communicated her concern and asked more questions than he had answers to.

Xavier drew in a breath. "Gracie will be fine, Dad. She's sad because—" What was he supposed to call her? "Emmy has to go away for a while."

"Oh." His mother's face fell. "You and Mackenzie had something special."

He'd thought the same, but their entire relationship had been a lie.

"Mackenzie has a boyfriend. His name's Cameron Grant."

Diane blinked at him. "The billionaire?"

Why wasn't he surprised she knew who Cameron was? His mother read the entertainment section of the papers the way some people read horoscopes.

Carl moved to stand beside his wife. "You're gonna have to explain yourself, son."

Xavier waved a hand at the couch. "Maybe you should sit down." He dropped into the armchair and leaned his arms against his thighs.

"I don't understand." His mother's brow furrowed. "She was dating both of you at once?"

If only.

"It's more complicated than that." Xavier squeezed his palms together. Sometimes you just had to blurt the truth out.

"Mackenzie has an identical twin named Madison. The woman I met, the one who was here last night, was Madison. She'd switched places with her sister and was pretending to be Mackenzie."

His mother's mouth fell open. "I thought those things only happened in movies."

His dad shook his head. "I don't understand, son. Why would she do that?"

"To get close to me."

"Is she a stalker?" Diane clung to his dad.

Having someone develop a fixation on you was never an ideal situation. But in this case, it would have been better for him if Madison had been a stalker. Then it would have been a matter for the police, not one he'd have to untangle himself. Or one with the possibility of shaking the foundations of his life.

"She wanted to get close to Gracie. Turns out Madison is Gracie's birth mom."

His parents gasped.

"I told you there was something special about Emmy." Gracie raced across the room to stand in front of him.

Uh-oh. This was not how he'd planned to tell Gracie about Madison's confession.

Would you have told her?

"Daddy, I told you my heart was connected to Emmy's."

Xavier had forgotten.

"Alana Grace, why are you out of bed?"

"I couldn't sleep, so I came to ask you to read a bedtime story."

This was his fault. If he'd waited until she'd fallen asleep to tell his parents what had happened, he wouldn't have to deal with this now.

"Does that mean we'll see Emmy again?"

His daughter's big, pleading eyes made him want to say yes. Almost. However, he couldn't help but wonder if, now that Alicia was dead, Madison could sue for custody of her child. He'd have to find out.

"Nothing has changed, Alana Grace. Now go back to bed."

Gracie's bottom lip trembled at his harsh tone. Why was this happening to him? He and Gracie had just started getting along. This was all Madison's fault. If she hadn't disrupted his perfect world, he wouldn't be on the verge of losing everything now.

Except his world hadn't been perfect in a long time. Besides, if not for Madison's intervention, he'd still be floundering as he figured out the basics of caring for his child. Why did life have to be so complicated?

Twenty-Five

Chapter 25

Madison trailed through the shop floor, cataloging the scene, not as someone with personal stakes, but as a stranger. Her sister had done a fantastic job of showcasing each item of furniture. She'd arranged them in much the same way as they'd have been in someone's home.

Mackenzie had added small accessories—pieces that looked like they belonged to someone. A vase of flowers. Photographs. A stack of letters on an end table. The result was inviting. Maybe Dad wouldn't be that upset.

"Oh, good. You're here."

Madison whirled at the feminine voice with a hand clapped over her heart.

The middle-aged woman laughed. "I'm sorry. Did I frighten you?"

Madison scanned the woman from her ponytail to her pink sneakers. "A little."

"I'm sorry." The woman repeated. "I've been jogging past this place for a couple of days. This is not my normal route, you understand?" She laughed. "I extended my jog for the holidays." She patted her flat stomach.

"Anyway, there's an entryway table in the display. I wanted to purchase it for my husband, but when I come later in the day, you're never open."

"That's because we're closed until after the new year."

"Oh." The woman's face fell. "Could you make an exception and sell me one teeny tiny thing?" She clasped her hands together. "Tomorrow's my anniversary, and that entryway table is the perfect gift for my Stuart, who's been searching for one like that."

Madison shrugged. "Sure."

It's not like she had a bunch of stuff doing, anyway. Besides, since Mackenzie had organized the shop floor, she was back to having too much time to think.

By the time Madison had rang up the sales for Muffy, who'd bought not only the entryway table but also a writing desk, someone else was trying to catch her attention.

Where had these antique lovers been in the last several years? Had they always lived in Cinnamon Hill? Surely, something as simple as rearranging the storeroom wasn't the reason their walk-in traffic had increased, was it?

"What in the filigree is happening here?"

Madison's head snapped up at the booming voice as she rang up the most recent customer.

"Dad? Mom? What are you doing here?" Madison completed the transaction and rushed to hug her parents. "Weren't you guys supposed to be in tomorrow?"

"We were." Robert Porter groused. "Until the cruise line

switched ports at the last minute." He propped his hands on his hips, head swiveling as he inspected the store.

"What's going on here? I knew we shouldn't have gone on that trip and left these children by themselves. They've been up to no good."

"Now, Bob," Margaret Porter rested a hand on his arm. "I always told you the store could use some freshening up."

Bob narrowed his eyes. "If it was good enough for my grandfather, it's good enough for me and should be for the rest of you."

Margaret spun in a slow circle. "This place almost feels like a home." She inhaled deeply. "What's that smell? It reminds me of Christmas."

"It's cinnamon spice." Madison had plugged in a diffuser and added the fragrance as per her sister's instructions.

"It's lovely." Margaret patted Madison's cheek.

"It wasn't me. It was Mackenzie."

"Hmph." Bob scowled. "That girl's been after me to change this, that, or the other since she was old enough to talk. Now we'll have people loitering and taking up valuable space."

"It's a good move, Daddy." She'd had her doubts in the beginning. "The customers like it." Madison named the figure she'd earned just that morning.

Her mother gaped. "That's more than we made last month."

Madison nodded. And most of that had been from restoration. Her father stroked his chin.

"Well, let's keep it this way for a while, test out this theory. Now it's time to go home. This store is closed for the rest of the year and that's final."

Madison kept her mouth shut. Her father wouldn't budge from his point. She'd won a major battle, getting him to admit what Mackenzie had always maintained—that they'd be a lot more profitable if they modernized the store.

She cast a glance over her shoulder as she followed her parents out the door. Maybe she could convince her father to replace the manual cash register.

* * *

At least the house was no longer silent.

"How was your trip?" Madison leaned against the sink while her mother puttered around the kitchen, making a list.

"It was wonderful." Maggie scribbled something on her notepad before turning to her. "Your father will complain, but he enjoyed every second."

Madison smiled. She was used to her dad's bluster.

"How are you, honey?" Her mother dropped the notepad and pen on the counter. She placed a palm on Madison's cheek and peered into her eyes. "You've been crying."

How had her mother figured that out?

"Did you and Mackenzie have a fight?"

Madison couldn't meet her mom's eyes. "Why'd you ask?"

Maggie quirked a brow. "The only time you two spend Christmas apart is when one of you is out of the country."

She jerked a shoulder. "Yes, well, maybe now that we're older, things have changed."

A fact she'd need to get used to if her sister never forgave her.

"The two of you will work things out, eventually."

Madison's eyes filled with tears. "What if Mackenzie doesn't forgive me?"

"Oh, Emmy." Maggie pulled Madison into her arms. "Your

sister loves you. Just give her a few days. You'll see." Maggie rubbed circles on Madison's back.

"I did something terrible, Mom. I don't think any of you will forgive me."

Maggie pulled away. "Madison?" She frowned. "What did you do?"

The worst thing ever. She'd betrayed her parents' upbringing. She'd lied to them, and kept a secret for years, depriving them of the right to know their only grandchild.

"I—"

"Maggie!"

Madison and her mom jerked at her father's bellow.

"Bob?"

Maggie was halfway across the kitchen when Bob stomped through the door.

"Some fool is outside claiming to be the father of Madison's child."

Twenty-Six

Chapter 26

Xavier was bleary-eyed the next day. Fear of making the wrong decision had made sleeping impossible. He stumbled into the kitchen, attracted by the smell of pancakes.

"Hey, Mom." He leaned down to kiss her cheek. "Thanks for making breakfast."

"No prob." She gestured to the island. "Sit, and I'll get your breakfast. I'm sure your dad will be here in a second. That man has a knack for timing my cooking."

Diane turned off the flame and slid the batch of pancakes onto a plate. She made quick work of plating three servings, complete with a healthy dose of syrup and fresh fruit.

The kitchen door swung open as she returned the orange juice to the fridge. His mom raised a brow.

"What did I tell you?"

"Hmm, something smells good." Carl hugged his wife from

behind, nibbling her neck until she giggled.

He wanted to be loved like that. His relationship with Alicia had been wonderful, but it had ended too soon. Had that been God's way of saying Xavier was to remain single for the rest of his life?

Better to marry than to burn.

Yeah, yeah.

Xavier rolled his eyes. "Why don't you two get a room?" He stabbed a bite of pancake. "Some of us aren't fortunate enough to be lucky in love." He shoved the food into his mouth. What had possessed him to speak to his parents that way?

"Oh, honey." Sorrow filled his mom's eyes. "We're sorry."

Carl waited until his wife sat before doing the same. "Have you thought about what you're going to do?"

Xavier nodded. He'd done nothing but think about it.

"And?" Carl met his gaze.

"I don't know, Dad." Xavier put down his fork, no longer hungry.

"Have you prayed about it, son?"

Had he? There'd been a few ambulance prayers, but had he sat in communion with God and poured out his concerns to his Heavenly Father?

"Not really."

"Why don't we do that now?" Carl held both hands out to his family.

Xavier gripped one hand as his mother did the same, completing the circle.

"Abba Father," Carl began. "Forgive us for not coming to You first with our problem. Xavier needs to know how to proceed in this situation with Emmy and Gracie.

"His first instinct is to pull away because he's hurt. But God,

You know why You allowed Emmy to be a part of Xavier and Gracie's lives. Only You know the plans you have for them.

"Clear everything from Xavier's mind except what he should do next according to Your will. Amen."

The Washingtons sat for a few moments, hands still linked, allowing the Holy Spirit to commune with them.

Xavier wanted to hold on to his anger against Madison, but in the silence, it ebbed away. Madison had lied to them, she'd deceived them all. That was on her. What happened next would be on him. Did he want to be the first man to break his daughter's heart?

* * *

It took Xavier the better part of an hour to convince Mackenzie he meant her sister no harm. It was another ten minutes before he'd coaxed the address to their parents' house out of her.

After a short debate about whether to leave Gracie with his parents, he'd decided to take her with him. This visit affected her life, too.

What Xavier hadn't counted on were two extra companions. He gripped Gracie's hand as he lifted her into the SUV.

"You didn't have to do this. We'd have been fine on our own."

Though it had been nice flying in a private plane instead of driving as he'd intended.

Cameron slid into the driver's seat after seating Mackenzie in the front. "It's fine." Cameron squeezed Mackenzie's hand. "I've gotten used to shuffling this one around. Besides, if I stick around until tomorrow, I'll meet my future in-laws."

Xavier's eyes widened. Cameron and Mackenzie were getting married?

Mackenzie snickered. "Behave. He'll believe you're serious."

"I'm putting you on notice because I know what I want." Cameron's voice was sincere.

The couple's obvious affection for each other created a pang of loneliness in him. He craved that again. Xavier dropped his gaze to Gracie, who was frowning at the back of Mackenzie's head.

"Gracie?" He brushed a hand over her hair to capture her attention. "Are you okay?"

"She looks just like Emmy, Daddy, but she doesn't make my heart feel the way it does with Emmy."

Mortification washed over him. "I'm sorry." His eyes lifted to Mackenzie, who had twisted to look at Gracie. "We're still working on keeping our inside thoughts in."

Gracie peered up at him. "Was that mean?"

"Uh—"

"That depends." Mackenzie cut in. "How does Emmy make your heart feel?"

Gracie scrunched up her nose. "Like a pile of chocolate kisses after Aunt Jacqui melts them to put them in a cake."

"Oh-kay." Mackenzie drew the word out. "How do I make your heart feel?"

"Less squishy. Like the chocolate is about to melt, but hasn't finished."

Mackenzie grinned. "That doesn't hurt my feelings. In fact, that's one of the nicest things anyone has ever said to me."

Gracie beamed. Xavier exhaled in relief. Maybe expanding Gracie's family wouldn't be a bad thing.

The vehicle stopped in front of a two-story blue and white house with a beautiful garden. His stomach churned. What if Madison refused to speak to him?

"Is it okay if Gracie stays with you for a few minutes while I speak with Madison?"

"Of course." Mackenzie climbed into the backseat and crooked her finger. "I'll do what I can to melt Gracie's heart chocolate into a goo."

Xavier stepped out of the vehicle, confident Gracie would be fine. He pushed a breath through his mouth.

Lord, I fear that I'm walking into a lion's den.

Yea, though I walk through the valley of the shadow of death, I will fear no evil: for thou art with me. Thy rod and thy staff they comfort me.

The words of the familiar psalm washed over him, bringing a sense of peace.

Okay, God. We can do this.

Xavier climbed the stairs and knocked on the bright blue door. The door swung inward and a barrel-chested man with a bald head scowled up at him.

"Yes?" The man's voice was brusque.

Xavier's voice box tightened. Hadn't Mackenzie said she did not expect her parents back until the next day? He wasn't prepared to meet this man. Madison's father. Gracie's grandfather.

"Spit it out, boy. What do you want?"

"Uhm," Xavier shook his head. "Is Ma-Madison here?"

The scowl deepened until Xavier had to lock his knees, not to step back. If this was the way Robert Porter responded to a stranger on his front porch, no wonder Madison had found it difficult to tell him about her pregnancy. His heart filled with compassion for her.

It must have been difficult to be pregnant in a strange country all by herself. She'd had to make the best choice for her child when she was little more than a teenager herself.

"Forever Furnished is closed until after the new year. Come to the office with photos of the piece you want Madison to restore for you." Mr. Porter grabbed the edge of the door. "With all respect, young man, the rest of this year is for family."

Xavier straightened until he towered over Mr. Porter. "I am family."

Robert Porter smirked. "I have one son." His gaze panned Xavier from head to toe. "You're not him."

Xavier drew in a breath. "No, sir. I'm the father of Madison's child."

"You're the what?" Robert Porter jutted out his chest. "Stay there." The door slammed in Xavier's face.

Well, that had not gone the way he'd anticipated.

Twenty-Seven

Chapter 27

Madison's head snapped up at her father's words. "Xavier's here?"

Did that mean he'd reconsidered? Would he allow her to see Gracie? Her heart pounded in her ears. Was there hope for them, after all? She turned toward the living room.

"Now wait just one minute." Her father stepped into her path. "Who is that man, and what is he talking about?"

"Daddy." Madison squeezed her eyes shut. She'd hoped she'd have more time to process and resolve the pain of confessing to Xavier and Mackenzie before she had to bare her soul again.

"Why is he claiming to be the father of your child?" Bob's voice got louder. "Madison, are you pregnant?"

"No." The word exploded from her mouth as her eyes flew open. "I'm not pregnant, but I should talk to Xavier before he changes his mind."

Bob folded his arms across his chest. "I'm not moving until I get some answers."

"Mom." She cast a pleading look at her mother.

"Does this have anything to do with what you were telling me earlier?"

She nodded, shame coursing through her.

Bob glared at his wife. "You knew about this?"

Maggie placed a hand on her husband's arm. "I know little more than you do. Bob, if we don't give the girl space to do what she needs to do, we'll never find out what's going on."

Maggie eyed Madison with such open compassion she teared up.

"She's a grown woman, Bob. That means she can make her own choices, including a few mistakes."

"Alright," Bob grumbled as he shuffled out of the way. "But I'm right behind you." He thrust a finger at her. "If that bearded beanpole hurts you, he'll have to deal with Bob Porter." He drew himself up to his full five feet eleven inches.

"Thanks, Daddy." Madison hugged her father, taking a moment to inhale his familiar scent of leather and linseed oil.

She'd made the wrong decision, hadn't she? If she'd been brave enough to tell her family what had happened in Italy, this scenario would have played out six years earlier.

Her father would have gotten angry, and her sister would have been hurt, but eventually, they'd have smoothed it over and moved on with their lives. She wouldn't have missed out on five years of her daughter's life.

All things worked together for the good of those who love the Lord and are called unto His purpose.

"I'm sorry, Daddy." Her tears splashed onto his sweater. "I love you and never meant to hurt you."

She pulled out of his embrace and hurried to speak with Xavier. At the door, Madison hesitated, resting one palm on the wooden surface.

She couldn't do this. Was she ready to be a mother? She'd ached for her daughter every day of the last five years, but did that mean she was prepared to be an active part of Gracie's life? What if Xavier was there to tell her to stay away from him and Gracie?

God, I can't do this.

The words wrenched out of Madison's spirit.

I'll be with you.

The still small voice washed over her.

When you pass through the waters, I will be with you; and when you pass through the rivers, they will not sweep over you. When you walk through the fire, you will not be burned; the flames will not set you ablaze.

The words of her favorite passage of Scripture filled her mind as her tears fell. Why would God walk with her when she'd as good as told Him she wanted nothing to do with Him?

"Madison?" Her mother laid a hand on her shoulder. "You'll make yourself sick."

Madison allowed her mom to fold her into a hug.

"Come now," Bob's voice was gruff with emotion. "None of this crying stuff."

He enfolded both women in his arms. "If he makes you cry this much, he's not worth it."

"It's not him." She pulled back and swiped at her cheeks. "I did something foolish. Mackenzie's mad at me. Xavier hates me, and I'll never see Gracie again."

"Gracie?"

Madison shook her head at her mother's soft question. "I'll

explain everything later, even though it will break your hearts."

Maggie rested both hands on Madison's shoulders. "You'll never do anything we can't love you through."

"Why?" Her eyes filled again.

"The same way we can't do anything to escape the love of God." Maggie brushed the tears from Madison's cheeks. "Your father feels the same way, though he'll never admit it."

Bob scowled. "Of course, I'll love her, Maggie. She's my girl." Bob turned his scowl on her. "You know that, right?"

She did now. How could she have doubted her dad's love or his willingness to forgive her for making a mistake? Had she done the same thing to God?

Bob's frown deepened. "Madison? You know I'll always love you, right? I may get angry because you do something I think is wrong, but I'll never stop loving you."

The same way God hadn't stopped loving her, even when she'd refused to take her hard stuff to Him.

Forgive me, Abba. Thanks for not leaving me alone.

"I know that now, Daddy." She pressed a kiss to her father's cheek. "Remember that. Whatever you find out today."

* * *

"Xavier?" He was already halfway down the steps, heading toward a black SUV.

He whirled, grabbing the rails when he almost fell. "Madison?"

"Yes."

He bounded up the stairs and stared down at her. "I didn't think you were coming out."

"Yeah. Why are you here?"

Xavier brushed his thumbs against her cheeks. "You were crying. I'm sorry."

Madison wanted to lean into his caress. To pretend for one moment, her lies hadn't severed the connection they'd developed in Orange Valley. But he was not hers. She took a step back.

"Why did you come? And how did you know where I lived?"

"Mackenzie gave me your address."

She arched a brow. Had she damaged their relationship to the point her sister wouldn't take a second to send her a text so she could have braced herself to face him?

"Is there somewhere private where we can talk?" His glance flickered to something behind her. "I'm not sure if your father has a gun, but he's angry enough to kill me with his bare hands."

"Uhm," she glanced back at her parents. Her dad glowered at Xavier, her mother's hand on his arm the only thing holding him back. "Sure." She gestured down the steps. "Let's go into the backyard."

She'd helped her father build the back deck when she and Mackenzie had been in high school, creating the perfect space for a barbecue or a family gathering. Usually, it was Madison's favorite place. Not today. Now she just wanted Xavier to say why he'd driven all the way to Cinnamon Hill so she could go back to healing her wounds.

"Please," she wrapped her arms around herself. "Can you tell me why you came?"

Chapter 28

Madison's husky voice raked up all the emotion he thought had died with her deception. Her swollen eyes tore at his gut. He'd done that.

Sure, she shouldn't have misrepresented who she was, but he should have handled it with more finesse. He should have been more willing to listen and less harsh in passing down judgment.

"How old were you when you had Gracie?"

Madison jerked as if he'd struck her. "You came all this way to ask me that?"

"Uh—"

"Never mind." She held up a hand. "I was twenty."

He'd already been married two years at that age, but he and Alicia had agreed not to have children until they'd finished college.

"It must have been hard being pregnant in a foreign country

with no support."

Her lips trembled. "It was." She lifted damp eyes to him. "Xavier, you're killing me here. If you made this trip to confirm that I feel terrible about what happened, let me admit it.

"Yes. I feel horrible about lying to you and Gracie, and even more for the pain my family will go through because of what I did—"

"Was it all a lie?"

"What?"

He stepped closer, shrinking the space between them to a hairsbreadth. "Was everything a ruse or did you-did you actually…"

He trailed off because he wasn't sure what he'd do if she'd been pretending the whole time. Not when his feelings for her were more real than anything he'd experienced since Alicia's death.

"No." Her tongue darted out to moisten her lips. "It wasn't all a lie. My feelings for you are as real as the ones I have for Gracie."

Xavier exhaled a sigh of relief.

"I really didn't plan to approach you. All I wanted was a glimpse of you and Gracie from a distance. Just to see her, you know?" She lifted a trembling hand to her mouth.

"Why now?"

He and Alicia had chosen not to keep Gracie's adoption status from her. But Madison showing up had thrown everything into a tailspin. He should have had years before he had to worry about what he'd do if Gracie wanted to meet her birth mother.

"I have PCOS. My doctor basically told me having a child was impossible. Mackenzie and I had always planned to become mothers about the same time and drive our husbands up the wall."

She shrugged. "I may have gone a little crazy when I realized that wouldn't happen. I'm sorry."

"It's okay. I understand."

The corner of her lips quirked. "Do you?"

"Okay. Maybe not, but I want to." He ran his eyes over her face, tracing the path he'd follow with his hands if things had been different.

Xavier drew in a breath and stepped back. "Gracie should know her birth mother and spend time with your family. If-if—"

Her eyes filled with tears. "If what?"

"If you can make peace with the idea that Alicia's family remains part of her life."

"Of course." Madison nodded, the tears spilling down her cheek. "They're her grandparents. I never expected…" She shook her head. "I expected nothing. Thank you."

He nodded, curling his hands into fists so he wouldn't pull her into his arms.

God, why did You put this woman into my life with this huge barrier between us?

"What about," her hands fluttered between them, "us?"

Sometimes, being an adult sucked. "For now, we focus on Gracie."

"I understand."

Did she? Because he didn't. He wanted to make his daughter happy, but not at the cost of his own happiness, and saying no to Madison hurt.

"Maybe we should go back inside." Madison cleared her throat. "I still haven't told my parents what happened. As far as they're concerned, you got me pregnant and are shirking your responsibility."

Xavier's eyes widened. "No wonder your father's furious at me."

"Are we doing this together?" She met his gaze. "You don't have to. You've already done more than I'd expected."

"Or we can introduce them to Gracie and let her charm them into being nice to me."

"She's here?" Madison's eyes darted to the space beyond his left shoulder, searching for Gracie.

"You didn't think she'd let me leave her behind, did you?"

He followed Madison to the SUV. Gracie would be ecstatic to see her again. The back door flew open as they approached, and Gracie barreled out into Madison's ready arms.

"Emmy!"

"Hi, Alana Grace." Madison swept her into her arms.

"I knew we'd see each other again." Gracie pulled back to peer into Madison's face. "Daddy says you're my birth mommy, is that true?"

"Yes, sweetie."

Gracie patted Madison's face. "I'm not mad. Daddy explained that sometimes birth mommies gift their babies to other mommies."

Madison's grateful eyes met his. "That's right. Sometimes they're not able to take care of their babies as well as they'd like to."

"Okay." Gracie rested her head against Madison's. "I love you, Emmy, almost as much as I love Aunt M'kenzie."

"What in the filigree is going on here?"

Oh, boy. Xavier turned to face the irate man in the driveway. Gracie needed to work her magic real fast.

Car doors slammed as Mackenzie and Cameron joined the

gathering in the front yard.

"Why don't we take this inside?" Once again, Cameron took control of the situation.

"Who the devil are you?" Mr. Porter growled up at him.

"Cameron Grant, sir."

"The real estate developer?"

"Yes, sir."

"Why are you at my house?"

Cameron met the older man's gaze. "I'm dating your daughter."

"Madison?" Confusion flooded Robert Porter's features.

Cameron grinned. "No, sir, Mackenzie." Cameron extended a hand, which Mr. Porter took, if Xavier had to guess, more out of politeness than anything else. "Nice to meet you, sir."

Mr. Porter harrumphed. "Go on one cruise and when you come back, everything's different. People changing around the store and having babies, strange men in my yard." He stomped away, still muttering.

Mackenzie glanced at her sister. "I take it he's been to the store?"

"He has." Madison rolled her eyes. "He started complaining about people loitering because if it was good enough for his grandpa..."

"It should be good enough for us." Both women completed the quote in an authentic imitation of their father's voice, then grinned at each other. Gracie's grin.

His eyes darted between the three of them. Same full lips. Same pert nose. Even the shape and color of their eyes were similar.

Wow. Xavier shook his head. How had he never noticed how much his daughter resembled Madison?

"Uncanny, isn't it?" Cameron asked.

"Extremely."

"In another few years," Cameron continued, "Gracie will look almost exactly like Madison and Mackenzie."

Maybe. Though Madison and Mackenzie were identical twins, he detected slight differences in their features.

Cameron lowered his voice. "The question is, if they dressed exactly alike, can you differentiate your girl from mine? Because I can assure you, your ability to do that has an enormous impact on whether you and Madison will be more than co-parents to Gracie."

Cameron ambled away. He took Mackenzie's hand and strolled toward the house before Xavier could form a denial or demand an explanation.

Twenty-Nine

Chapter 29

Madison stared after Mackenzie and Cameron. Her sister had met a man who treated her like the princess she was. But it was a bittersweet moment for her.

The chasm between her and Mackenzie was so wide that she didn't get to share this moment with her. There were no tidbits about the sweet things Cameron had done or details about how her sister felt about him.

The wise woman builds her house, but the foolish pulls it down with her hands.

She'd been the foolish woman of Proverbs. Her lies and deception had destroyed her most treasured relationship. She cut her gaze to Xavier. Maybe even stole the future she craved.

Xavier's concerned gaze met hers. "Will things be okay between you two?"

"I don't know. We've never gone through anything like this

before."

"It'll be okay, Emmy." Gracie patted her cheek. "Aunt M'kenzie's heart is tangled up with yours. You'll see."

Madison frowned. What did Gracie mean? Was she hinting that Mackenzie missed her?

"Here." Xavier reached for Gracie. "Let me take the junior prophet from you." He settled her against his side. "I'm not sure how she knows these things, but I'd believe her. Gracie told me she had a connection to you before you explained who you were."

When Madison and Xavier walked into the living room, Mackenzie and Cameron were sitting on one end of the sofa. Mr. Porter glared at them across the coffee table. Mrs. Porter perched on the armrest, a hand on his shoulder.

"It's sweet, Bob, the way he came to check on her."

"Everything's sweet for you, Maggie, because you've got babies on the brain." He growled at Mackenzie. "Next thing, this one will tell us he knocked her up, too."

"Daddy!" Mackenzie folded her arms across her chest. "This is the reason Madison didn't tell us anything—because you're always growling at us." Mackenzie threw her hands into the air.

"Oh, you know your father, dear. He's more growl than bite."

"Yeah, that's difficult to live with when you make a mistake." Mackenzie's eyes met hers over their father's head.

Did that mean her sister had forgiven her?

"Put me down, Daddy." Gracie's voice rang out in the silence after Mackenzie's statement.

Her parents turned in their direction as Gracie padded toward them.

"Bob." Maggie's hand flew to her mouth.

Gracie went up to Bob until her face was inches away from his. The two stared at each other. What was running through her parents' minds? Would they notice the similarities between Gracie and herself at that age?

Gracie nodded and patted Bob's cheek. "I wasn't going to like you because you were shouting at Emmy, but I changed my mind. I think you use your shouty voice because you love people so much you can't be quiet."

Xavier choked. Madison stole a glance at him. Was he laughing?

"Alana Grace."

"It's the truth, Daddy. You always say I should tell you where it hurts instead of being grumpy."

Xavier's shoulders shook. Yes, definitely laughing. And why not? Gracie had said what Madison had thought many times. Her father's gruff demeanor made it difficult for her to share what was in her heart.

It was why she and her father mostly communicated during a restoration project. Their shared love for bringing a neglected piece back to life had cemented their relationship. But it hadn't made confessing her pregnancy or the decision she'd made to give Gracie up any easier.

"Who are you?" Bob's voice was full of wonder.

"Bob, she's the spitting image of our girls," Maggie spoke with the same awe that filled Bob's voice.

Madison went to stand behind Gracie.

"Mom, Dad," she rested her hands on Gracie's shoulders, drawing strength from the lean frame. "I'd like you to meet my daughter, Alana Grace."

"You and him," Bob jabbed a finger at Xavier who stood beside her, "had a baby?"

She cut her eyes at Xavier. How much of the story had he told Gracie?

"Not exactly." She cleared her throat. "Gracie was born in Italy." Her parents' eyes widened as the implications hit. "Xavier and his wife adopted Gracie as a baby."

"You're married?"

"Where's your wife now?"

Maggie and Bob spoke, their words blending into each other.

"My wife, Alicia, died three years ago."

"I'm sorry for your loss." Maggie offered her condolences with compassion.

Bob stood. "I need to—" he shook his head. "Everybody sit. Maggie, come with me." Bob stomped toward the front door.

"We'll be back in a minute." Maggie waved a hand. "Make yourself comfortable." She hurried after her husband.

"Well," Cameron broke the silence. "After a conversation like that, I could eat a slice of cake."

"With ice cream?" Gracie's hopeful voice made everyone chuckle.

"Madison." Mackenzie came to stand before her. "I get why you didn't tell Dad or Mom." Everything they told their mother made it in some shape or form to their dad. "I wish…"

Mackenzie's unsaid words filled the silence.

Why hadn't Madison trusted her enough with her secret? If she'd told Mackenzie what had happened, they could have walked through it together.

"I'm sorry. I should have told you what I was going through. Then maybe—" Madison spread her palm wide.

Mackenzie fitted her hand into Madison's. "Let's not fight anymore. We can't go back and change the past. All we can do is live with our choices and make the best of it from now on.

"For better or worse," Mackenzie spread her arms to include the others. "We're in this together. Let's walk the path set before us."

163

Thirty

Chapter 30

Xavier marveled at Mackenzie's words and her capacity for forgiveness. Though Madison's actions had hurt her, she was doing the hard work of pressing into the next phase of their lives—whatever that may be. Gracie could learn a lot from her aunt.

If it had been up to him, he'd still be in Orange Valley, brooding over Madison's deception and struggling to interpret her every action and word. His mother's prompting, and Gracie's love for Madison, had forced him into action.

He'd made the right choice. He sighed. Thank God. The front door opened, and the Porters returned at about half the speed at which they'd left, their faces set in solemn lines. Had he celebrated too early?

Mr. and Mrs. Porter stood united on one side of the room. Thanks to Mackenzie's speech, everyone else was also standing. If this had been a superhero movie, it would have appeared to be an uneven standoff.

Bob Porter met the gaze of each of them before he spoke.

"This is what's going to happen next. Since I'm pretty sure the full story is not one suitable for delicate ears, you'll tell us the details later."

"You can tell us after dinner." Mrs. Porter added in a soft voice.

"You two," Bob Porter skewered him and Cameron with his gaze. "Will be our guests for the next couple of days."

Xavier's eyes flittered to Madison. What was her father doing? He assumed Xavier and Madison were having an affair, so he stuck them under the same roof together?

Mr. Porter's eyes narrowed. "You'll stay in the apartment over the garage."

"Actually," Cameron cleared his throat. "I have a house not too far from here. I inherited it from my uncle Ezra after he died."

Mrs. Porter's eyes sharpened. "You're related to Ezra Murray?"

"Yes. He was my mother's older brother."

Mrs. Porter nodded. "Good to know."

Cameron smiled his million-dollar smile, the one he wore in every picture Xavier had ever seen of him.

"Rather than put you out of your way, Xavier and I can stay there."

"You'll stay in the apartment over the garage." Mr. Porter raised a hand. "I understand that you're used to doing things a certain way. But this is my house and these are my girls. If you want to date one of my daughters, you'll stay in the apartment."

"Daddy!" Mackenzie glared at her father. "This isn't the Dark Ages."

"Maybe not, but those are my rules."

Xavier raised a finger. "I'm not dating any of your daughters, sir."

Bob Porter threw his head back and laughed. The action was so surprising, all Xavier could do was blink. As quickly as it started, Bob Porter's hilarity disappeared.

"You must think I'm stupid, son. You may not be the biological father of Madison's child, but I've seen the way you look at her. I was not there to protect her last time, but I won't fail her again."

"Dad." Madison was on the verge of tears.

"Seriously, Dad, you can't expect everyone to scrap all their plans to move into your house. They don't have any clothes. No change of underwear." Mackenzie threw up her hands. "No toothbrush."

Bob's expression was long-suffering. "I know that Mackenzie. I'm not unreasonable."

Xavier stifled a snort.

"They can go back to wherever they came from and return with their clothes. Tomorrow."

Did this man believe he was some kind of king who could enforce his will on others? Xavier had a life. He had things to do back at his house. He couldn't pick up and move to Cinnamon Hill—even if it was temporary.

Not after his parents had traveled to Orange Valley to visit him. And he was supposed to just leave them to kowtow to Bob Porter's desire for redemption?

Even though Bob had shot him down the last time, Xavier stuck his hand up.

Mr. Porter sighed. "What is it, son?"

"My parents are visiting me for a few days—"

"They're welcome to join us here."

Xavier tilted his head. "Mr. Porter—"

"Since we're practically family, you can call me Bob."

"Thank you. Bob, you expect my parents to move into your apartment above the garage?"

Just how big was that apartment?

Bob shook his head. "No. Your parents will stay in the main house with the rest of the family. It's the two of you who'll be staying above the garage."

Okay. This man was being unreasonable.

"No, thanks."

Gracie tugged on his shirt. "I wanna stay, Daddy."

"I'm not forcing anyone to be here." Bob met his gaze and then Cameron's. "I'm just doing what I think is best. We've seen the damage keeping secrets can wreak on a family.

"We can continue to walk down the path of division and dissension. Or we can make a choice to forge a fresh path and move forward."

The man had pretty much echoed Mackenzie's words. Who were these people and how could he become more like them?

"Maybe we should have said it this way." Mrs. Porter gave her husband a side-eye. "Cameron, Xavier, we're inviting you to spend a few days with our family. We'd like to get to know the men who've taken such interest in our daughters." She beamed at Gracie. "And we'd love to spend some time with our granddaughter."

When phrased that way, he couldn't take offense.

Xavier looked at Bob Porter—really looked at him. Beyond the bluster and the gruff demeanor, he was a father protecting his daughter. One who'd recently learned how he'd failed to protect her in the past and had to deal with the fallout.

Xavier stroked his beard. Bob Porter was doing what any loving father would do. Besides, if Gracie had been in Madison's shoes, he'd have done worse.

"Has anyone prayed about this?" Cameron's words attracted everyone's attention.

"Of course." Bob's voice was brusque. "What did you think we were doing outside?"

Thirty-One

Chapter 31

To Madison's surprise, telling her parents what had happened was easier than she'd expected. Maybe because she'd already told the story to Mackenzie and Xavier. Or because Mackenzie sat beside her through the entire retelling, gripping Madison's hand.

Why had she thought she was better off keeping secrets from her sister? Madison made another pass in front of the window overlooking the front yard.

"You'll wear a hole in the floor," Mackenzie commented without turning her attention away from the Christmas movie she was watching.

"You don't understand."

"Explain it to me." Mackenzie muted the TV and patted the space beside her.

Madison plopped onto the couch and dropped her head into her hands. "The last time I saw the Washingtons, they believed

I was you."

"That isn't so bad." Mackenzie rubbed soothing circles on Madison's back. "I'm sure Xavier's already explained everything. It will be okay."

Madison snorted. "Easy for you to say. You're not the one who has to face the parents of the guy you like after lying to them."

"So you apologize, Madison." Mackenzie's voice was stern. Madison turned her head to peer up at her.

"You apologize to the Washingtons and move on with your life. At least Xavier's parents don't think you're a gold digger who's taking advantage of their son."

Madison's mouth fell open. "Are you serious?"

Mackenzie pressed her lips into a firm line and gave a single nod. "It doesn't matter. Cameron and I are ignoring it."

She was selfish. She'd instigated this whole thing for her benefit. And yes, her sister had fallen in love with Cameron because of their switch, but she'd also assumed things had been easy for Mackenzie.

"I'm sorry." Madison sat up and faced her twin. "I've been selfish this holiday. I'm sorry Cameron's parents don't realize how magnificent you are."

"Don't worry about me. Focus on surviving this impromptu house party with your baby daddy and future in-laws." Mackenzie winked. "Think of the stories you'll have to tell."

* * *

Things were going better than she'd expected. The Washingtons had accepted her apology and offered their forgiveness, determined to make the best of the situation.

Diane and her mother had bonded instantly. The two sat in one corner of the deck, heads close together like teenagers sharing secrets.

Cameron and Mackenzie cuddled on the long couch. Even her father and Carl were busy. Madison walked to the side of the house and wrapped her arms around herself.

"This is too hard, God. I'm not sure if I can do it."

What were the odds that she finally found a guy who intrigued her, but she couldn't be with him because she'd botched everything?

"Are you alright?"

"Xavier." Madison clapped a hand to her chest as he rounded the house.

"Sorry." His lips quivered. "I didn't mean to scare you. I saw you come this way and wondered if you'd like some company."

Yes. But not like this. She wanted to go back to the Madison and Xavier pre-confession. Before she'd ruined things with the man she'd been halfway in love with and almost lost the chance to be a part of her daughter's life.

"I'm fine." She tipped her lips upward into the semblance of a smile. "Don't worry about me."

He sighed. "You don't have to pretend with me."

"Hmph." She stared at a spot beyond his shoulder. "Are you sure?"

They really needed another spot to have heart-to-heart conversations. Maybe she'd coax her dad into building a gazebo at one end of the garden.

"I'm sure."

His expression was so earnest that she decided to risk baring her heart.

"You want to hear the truth? Here it is." She took a deep

breath. "This whole thing feels tenuous. I'm worried that one day I'll make you mad, and then I'll never see Gracie again until she's eighteen."

Hurt flickered in his eyes. "That's what you believe about me? That I'm someone who would keep you away from your child?"

"I don't know, Xavier." She wrapped her arms around herself.

"I came after you." He flung his arms out. "Twice."

"Yeah, well." She tilted her chin. "Would you have done that if your mother hadn't pushed you into doing it?"

His gaze flickered away. "Maybe."

She snickered. "Very convincing."

"I don't know. Okay?" He put his hands on his head. "I wish things weren't this complicated."

That made two of them.

"I wish things were different." His eyes caressed her face. "If only we were in the middle of the Christmas romance our daughter has imagined us in since the first moment she met you."

Her breath caught. Could Xavier be feeling the same way she was?

"I wish…" His voice trailed off.

She bit her bottom lip, and his eyes latched on to the motion.

"What do you wish, Xavier?" Her voice was breathy.

"I wish you wouldn't do that and that I could do it instead."

Oh, filigree.

Madison dragged a shaky hand through her hair. How was she supposed to respond to a statement like that? She closed her eyes to shut out the invitation in his.

What would Mackenzie do? Well, first off, her sister would never have been caught in this situation. If only there was a way for them to start over.

"Emmy—"

"Xavier—"

They both spoke at once.

"Go ahead." Xavier gestured for her to speak.

She straightened her shoulders. "We should start over."

Confusion flickered across his face. "What do you mean?"

Ask for what you want.

Her pesky inner voice chose the worst moments to pipe up. "Madison?"

She drew in a breath. "Am I misunderstanding you, Xavier? I sense that you want something more." She waved her hand between them. "Is that right?"

"Are you kidding?" Xavier's expression was incredulous.

"Oh." She took a step back. How embarrassing. It appeared the glimmer of interest he'd had for her disappeared when he found out she was Gracie's birth mother. "Never mind. I just thought—"

"Let me make it clear, Madison." Xavier tugged her into his arms. "So you don't misunderstand what I want." He lowered his head and claimed her lips.

Oh, my word. Heat rushed through her. Madison clutched his shoulders as the sensation threatened to sweep her off her feet.

Oh, my.

Xavier lifted his head, and a slow smile spread across his face. "Did that clarify things for you?"

"Hmm." She nodded. "Yes."

If he'd meant to thrust her heart into overdrive, he'd suc-ceeded. The man had kissed her until she'd forgotten what she'd wanted to say. She bit her bottom lip.

"Madison." Her name was almost a growl. "I'm sure I just demonstrated what that does to me."

He had. His heart was pounding as hard as hers.

"Sorry." She stepped out of his arms, though what she truly wanted was to cuddle closer and settle into his kisses.

"That was not the response I was expecting." He took a step toward her. Madison held up a hand.

"Stay there." She needed room to think, and being too close to Xavier clouded her senses. She walked backward until she bumped into the wall.

Xavier observed her, his eyes at half-mast. "Why are you running away, Madison?"

"Not running, just thinking."

She hated being practical. That's why Mackenzie always had to talk her down. But her sister had already secured her prince, and it was Madison's turn to do the same. When her heart rate was close to normal, she met his gaze.

"I still believe we need a do-over." She pushed away from the wall and stuck out her hand. "Hi. My name is Madison Porter and I have an identical twin sister named Mackenzie. We have an older brother named Robert Junior. We call him RJ. My brother does some secret job for the army."

She hauled in a breath. "I am the birth mother of a beautiful baby girl who I gave up for adoption five years ago."

What else should she disclose?

"Oh. I have PCOS. My doctor says it's unlikely that I'll ever have another child."

Well, he hadn't run away yet. She may as well continue.

"I'm halfway in love with you, Xavier, and would love the chance to fall all the way in."

She held her breath as she waited for his response. A slow

grin spread across his face, and her shoulders sagged in relief.

"Nice to meet you, Madison. My name's Xavier Washington. I'm a video game designer, who, until last week, hasn't had a new concept since his wife died three years ago. I'm the adoptive father of a beautiful five-year-old girl who's almost as beautiful as you."

He clasped her hands and electricity shot up her arms. "I'm halfway in love with you too and would like nothing more than the chance to fall all the way in."

Oh. Madison's heart sighed at Xavier's declaration. Maybe she'd get to keep her Christmas family after all.

Thirty-Two

Chapter 32

Xavier gazed with longing at Madison, who snuggled in a blanket fort on the living room floor with Gracie. What he wanted was a few minutes alone with Madison.

After a couple of days of almost living in the same house with her, he'd realized the only things she'd lied about had been her name and connection to Gracie. In every other way, she'd represented herself authentically to him.

He scanned the living room where every sofa and couch was occupied. The problem with being around seven other people constantly was the lack of privacy. They were never alone. He sighed.

If he could fast-forward the time, he would. Then it would be after dinner, and he and Madison would sneak away for some quiet conversation and a few stolen kisses.

Diane's gaze flickered to Maggie's before zooming in on him.

"You know what I'm craving?"

Xavier ran his gaze between the two older women. It amazed him how quickly they'd bonded. Hopefully, Maggie would get along with Alicia's parents as well.

"Xavier, I believe your mother's talking to you." His father's voice brimmed with amusement.

"Sorry." He shook his head. "What did you say, Mom?"

"I said, do you know what I'd like to eat right now?"

He frowned. Hadn't she said that before? Had she answered, and he'd missed it?

"No. What?"

"One of Regina's Christmas specialty cookies. Xavier, be a dear and get me a dozen."

What was his mother up to? Xavier cocked his head. "You want me to drive to Idlewood to buy you a dozen cookies?"

"Yes." His mother beamed at him. "I was telling Maggie about them earlier and she'd love to taste one."

"Oh, yes," Maggie perked up. "Diane says they're only available this time of the year."

"Buy a dozen of each of her specialty cookies." His mother continued. "May as well enjoy ourselves, since they won't be available again until next year."

"Yes," his dad chimed in. "Take Madison with you."

Xavier's gaze flitted to each person in the room as everyone's attention shifted to the weird conversation he was having with his mom.

"Okay." He stood and frowned at them. "Am I being pranked?"

"Dad-dy!" Gracie rolled her eyes at him. "We're trying to get you and Emmy to go away."

"What?" His gaze flitted to Madison, whose shoulders shook

with laughter.

"Yes, Daddy. The two of you are going on a long trip together and when you come back, you'll be in love."

"Is that so?" Xavier smirked. "All of you are in on this plan?"

He met Bob's gaze. The man hadn't given him an ounce of encouragement where Madison was concerned.

"Of course." Bob jabbed a finger at him. "My granddaughter needs two loving parents, living in the same house." Bob narrowed his eyes at him. "After they get married."

"Okay then." He extended a hand to Madison. "Our families want to get rid of us."

She slid her hand in his, and he grinned. Who knew all he had to do to get time alone with Madison was to have their five-year-old daughter arrange an intervention?

"What time should we be back?" He quirked a brow at Gracie, who appeared to be the brains behind the whole thing.

"Not until you're in love." Gracie made a shooing motion with her hands. "But come home before midnight or you'll both turn into pumpkins."

They made it all the way to the SUV before they burst out laughing. Madison turned and slipped her arms around his neck.

"Should we have told them we were already halfway in love with each other?"

"Halfway?" He lifted a brow. "I toppled over the halfway mark days ago." He tugged her closer to him. "How can I get you to join me on this side of love?"

"Hmm. I'm not sure." Her gaze dropped to his mouth. "How about we *not* drive to Idlewood, but don't return to the house until a few minutes before midnight?"

"What would we do until then?"

"I'm sure we'll figure out something." She tugged his head closer to hers just as his phone buzzed in his pocket. "Ignore it."

It was tempting not to answer it. "I can't. Suppose it's Gracie?"

Her eyes widened. "I didn't think about that. I'm a lousy mother."

"Stop." He wrestled the phone out of his pocket. "It takes a second to get used to always considering the needs of another little person." He glanced at the screen. "It's not Gracie."

"Who is it?"

He swiped to answer. "Noah."

"Your agent?" Madison mouthed the words.

He nodded. "What's up?"

He gripped Madison's hand as he waited for Noah's news.

"They loved the concept." His friend got straight to the point.

"Yeah?" Xavier gripped the phone tighter. Thank God.

"They wanna start talking about pre-production after the new year. You did good, my friend."

"Thanks, Noah." Not only for going to bat for him but also for sticking around when he was at his lowest. "For everything."

He disconnected the call, awestruck at the conversation and what it meant. A month ago, he'd believed God had abandoned him to walk through his pain alone. His gift was in shambles from misuse, he had no relationship with his child and had lost the woman he'd planned to spend the rest of his life with.

"Hey." Madison lay a hand on his chest. "You okay?"

He brushed his fingers down her cheek. "I was thinking about how much God has blessed me. A few weeks ago, I believed He'd left me to walk through my sorrows alone."

She tipped her head up to his. "And now your cup has

overflowed."

"Yes. How did you know?"

"I've gone through a similar thing. I was sure He'd abandoned me when I needed Him most, but He was with me all along. What did your agent want?"

"Noah starts pre-production talks for our video game next year."

"*Our* video game?"

"I wouldn't have come up with the idea without you."

"I'm not sure that's how it works, but I'm honored you'd credit me with the idea."

"I'd give you more than that." He slid his hands around her waist. "Madison, life can be fragile. I don't want to waste any more time pretending I'm not in love with you."

He cupped her face. "I love you, Madison, and I hope we can find a way to co-parent Gracie together. I want to walk through the rest of our time together as partners. Lovers."

Her eyes widened.

"Uh—" Why did he use that word? "I didn't mean lovers in the traditional sense. Not until after we…"

What was he saying? "I mean, not as the world uses that word, but—" What should he say to get out of this awkward situation?

Madison burst out laughing. "I know what you mean, Xavier. I love you, too, and I'd be honored to co-parent our daughter with you." She slid her hands up his chest. "I'd love to have my Christmas family all year round."

"Deal. We should seal our promise with a kiss."

"I can arrange that." She stood on tiptoe and pressed her lips to his.

He'd believed his season of loss would never end, but God

had other plans for him.

<h1 style="text-align:center;font-style:italic">Epilogue</h1>

One year later

RJ Porter traced his fingers over the surface of the custom invitation. Leave it to his twin sisters to fall in love in the same year and decide to have a double wedding. Who got married on Christmas Eve, the most expensive time of the year?

Of course, one of his sisters was marrying a billionaire and the other guy wasn't hurting for money, either.

He pushed away from his desk and dropped to the floor for push-ups. He barely made it to ten before he was trembling worse than a rookie in his first week of training.

Who knew a stab to the gut would have such a lingering effect on a person? And who wanted an undercover agent who couldn't do ten push-ups without whimpering? Because if he couldn't do that, how could he take on an enemy?

He got up and swiped the sweat from his forehead. The last place he wanted to be was around his family. He wouldn't enjoy his mom and sisters pulling or clucking at him. Nor would he enjoy the disappointment in his father's eyes because his only son had rejected the family business. As far as Robert Porter Senior was concerned, RJ had rejected him.

For a second, RJ considered not attending the wedding. Then he got a mental image of his sisters' faces as children, twin expressions of adoration and love. He couldn't—wouldn't—let them down, even if he no longer deserved their devotion.

It was a week-long destination wedding. Surely there was a corner in the villa where he could hide until the ceremony. He'd be there for his sisters and then he'd figure out what to do with the rest of his life if he couldn't be a soldier.

* * *

Will RJ find a new purpose for his life? Find out in A Wife for Christmas.

* * *

Did you enjoy Madison and Xavier's story? Sign up for my newsletter at https://tinyurl.com/AFFCBonus and get a bonus epilogue.

Author's Note

Thanks for reading Madison and Xavier's story.

When I first got the idea for a twin switch, Madison was going to be the "bad" twin. A bit of research soon showed me how twins (and triplets) hate that stereotype.

Instead, I gave Madison a secret—one that affected several people. Madison's secret is a reminder that sometimes we make poor choices. We keep things hidden that should have been exposed.

But, as those things always do, they will come to light.

I hope Madison's dilemma reminded you that sometimes the outcome we fear is less daunting in real life than it was in our heads.

My prayer for you is that the next time you have one of those life-changing decisions to make, you'll take a moment to consult with your Heavenly Father. And yes, I know God doesn't always give us instant answers.

Sometimes He does, and other times He speaks through godly people in our lives.

If you enjoyed spending time with this couple as much as I did, please consider sharing your thoughts about this book online, but please, no spoilers! Help me get this book to other readers who'll love it.

185

About the Author

Aminata Coote's love affair with books began with an upside-down copy of Silas Marner. She's passionate about helping women understand the truth of the Bible for themselves.

She writes stories and books that point to a God bigger than our failings and provides hope to others. Aminata is also the author of several Bible studies and devotionals.

She lives in Montego Bay, Jamaica with her husband and son.

Connect with her on her website, aminatacoote.com, or on Instagram or Facebook @aminatacoote. Learn more about her books at https://aminatacoote.com/books-by-aminata-coote/.

Sign up for Aminata's newsletter at https://tinyurl.com/AFFCBonus and get a bonus epilogue.

Other Books by the Author

Inspirational Contemporary Romance

Orange Valley Series
His Perfect Wife
His Perfect Match
His Perfect Family
His Perfect Choice

Christmas with the Porters
A Husband for Christmas
A Family for Christmas

The Firefighters of Orange Valley
Falling For Her Fake Wedding Date

Christian Living
Face Your Fear: Choose Faith Over Fear
Affirmations for Christian Women: Biblical Affirmations for
Spiritual and Emotional Self-Care
7 Lessons on Endurance from Hebrews 12:1-2

Through God's Eyes: Marriage Lessons for Women
Unwavering: How to Stand Strong in Your Faith

Learn more about my books at
https://tinyurl.com/ACooteBooks

Newsletter Sign-up

Sign Up for Aminata's Newsletter

Keep up to date with Aminata's latest news on book releases and events by signing up for her email list at https://tinyurl.com/AmiCReader.

Join Aminata's community

Website: https://aminatacoote.com

Facebook: https://www.facebook.com/AminataCoote

Instagram: https://www.instagram.com/aminatacoote/

Want more inspirational romance?

Check out the Orange Valley series.

His Perfect Wife

First love, second chances: Can they mend a broken heart?

Tonya McPherson once dreamed of marrying her first love, but four years after he left her, she's abandoned the idea of a fairy tale ending. Now he's back, and they're forced to work together. Can her heart withstand the constant "what-ifs"?

Malcolm Hall deeply regrets breaking up with Tonya. Assigned as the youth pastor at her church, he yearns for a second chance. Can Tonya find it in her heart to forgive him?

Is it too late for a fresh start, or will they let a once-in-a-lifetime love slip away?

His Perfect Match

Two unlikely lovers, battling financial woes.

Brianna McPherson, a struggling communications consultant, desperately needs paying clients, or her business will crumble.

Daniel Hutchinson's church faces imminent closure unless he can attract new members.

When their paths cross, sparks fly, and an unexpected love blossoms.

In the midst of their professional struggles, they find a love that could change everything.

His Perfect Family

A single mom fighting for her son, a second chance at love.

Gabrielle Wallace is a determined single mother fighting for custody of her son. Theodore McPherson was her first love, the man who'd ghosted her.

Theodore, a firefighter, seeks to make amends for letting Gabrielle go. When he learns she needs a husband to keep her son, he steps up as her groom, hoping to rekindle a lasting love.

Their journey is marked by hurdles and struggles. Can they overcome their past and find happiness together, or will differences tear them apart once more?

His Perfect Choice

She's given up on love, but he's determined to win her heart.

Jessica Smith's dream of being a pastor's wife shatters, testing her faith as she battles Guillain-Barré Syndrome. Her physical therapist, Andre Meyers, harbors years of unspoken love for her and seizes the opportunity to prove it.

Together, they face their past and learn that brokenness can lead to a beautiful future.

In this heartwarming tale of hope, faith, and second chances, will they take a chance on love for their happily ever after?